EMBRACE THE MAGIC

EMBRACE THE MAGIC

Caris Roane

Copyright © 2012 by Twin Bridges LLC

Formatting and cover by Bella Media Management.

ISBN:1494955350 ISBN-13: 978-1494955359

THE BLOOD ROSE SERIES
BOOK TWO

EMBRACE THE MAGIC

CARIS ROANE

Dear Reader,

EMBRACE THE MAGIC is the second installment of my paranormal romance series, called the Blood Rose series, based on the question: what would happen if only one woman could satisfy the blood-starvation needs of a powerful master vampire? From there, I built a world called the Nine Realms, linked to earth through 'realm access points', attached to various North American cities, in this case, Shreveport, Louisiana.

A master vampire rules each of the realms and **EMBRACE THE MAGIC** follows the path of Mastyr Ethan as he meets his blood rose, in the form of Samantha Favreau, a woman who has no idea she's half-fae, half-human.

I've enjoyed exploring and expanding the world of the Nine Realms, and in **EMBRACE THE MAGIC** I also asked the question: can guilt make it impossible for an individual to embrace love? Both Samantha and Ethan have reasons to feel guilty, but can they move beyond the past and reach for the future?

I hope you enjoy **EMBRACE THE MAGIC**, the sequel to **EMBRACE THE DARK**, which picks up three months after events that brought so much happiness to Mastyr Gerrod and Abigail. You'll meet Vojalie and Davido again and of course, their new baby, Bernice! Enjoy!

To learn more about Caris Roane and to sign up for her newsletter go to http://www.carisroane.com/

Chapter One

Mastyr Vampire Ethan stared down into Sweet Gorge where two of his Guardsmen hauled up a body on a sling carried between them. They flew side by side, matching their movements by long practice. The night air, though usually fresh in early April, carried a rancid edge, something he'd connected with this area for a long time.

But he'd lost another of his Guard here at Sweet Gorge, killed sometime this past week, but located by a search patrol just a half hour ago. And this was the fourth murder in a month.

Something was on the wind.

"Invictus?" Finn scratched behind his right ear. He was Ethan's second-in-command, his long red hair a beacon in any situation.

Using both hands, Ethan shoved his own unruly hair away from his face. Sweat dripped from his forehead. The temp wasn't too warm in Bergisson Realm this time of year, but when his blood-starvation reached difficult levels, he'd often perspire like he'd been battling for hours. "What the hell was Paul doing patrolling in this area?"

Ethan didn't know Paul well, but he felt responsible for him, as he did for all his Guard. He'd built his force to three hundred strong, but Paul, as a new recruit, wasn't well-known to many of the Guardsmen.

"He didn't have orders to go out here, not with three other Guardsmen dead in the past few months along the eastern border." Ethan let his gaze move from one end of the gorge to the other, then along the monolith to the east. A familiar heavy guilt clawed at his chest. This part of his realm was off-limits having been the place of a massacre forty years earlier.

"Maybe his body was dumped."

Ethan's frown tightened his forehead. "Most likely."

There was a connection between Sweet Gorge and the Invictus. He just didn't know what it was.

Sweet Gorge used to be a place of great beauty and had once been a modest resort, a place his family had been to a lot in its prime. Fae leadership had also met here often.

Now his mother, father and sister were gone, lost in the attack, along with many loved ones, over two hundred realm killed all at one time.

Afterward, the stream had dried up, the source cursed by a powerful fae of unknown ancestry. No one had seen the fae female or the deed, only that the stream was blocked and no amount of power had ever released it. A wall of crystals resided there and none of the fae he knew would go near it.

Besides, there was always the stench to warn realm-folk away, of something not right, very ancient, and deadly.

He glanced over the wooded ridgeline along the north ridge. A breeze picked up sending sharp pine scents through the air.

But something else struck his nostrils, the scent of dark fae magic, as though it waited there. His muscles flexed involuntarily along the insides of his arms. Yet in all these decades not a single fae of power, in any of the Nine Realms, had been able to figure out where all that power was coming from, not even Vojalie, the most powerful fae he knew.

He reset his long hair with the traditional woven clasp. He'd been flying through his realm for the past three hours, hunting the red wind of the Invictus, a sign that preceded an attack. He hadn't found anything yet, but the night was young.

He'd used up a lot of precious energy, however, and he needed to feed again, the bane of his station as a true mastyr vampire. All the mastyrs he knew experienced desperate levels of blood-need and lately, for no reason he could figure out, his starvation had worsened.

His mouth filled with saliva as he drew his cell from the pocket of his battle leathers. He sent a quick text to one of his *doneuses* and wasn't surprised at all when he got a message back to stop in for a quick tap. Bless the dozen women who serviced him.

Damn, he hurt, deep in his gut. He shifted away from Finn and took deep breaths as a couple of hard spasms pulled on his empty stomach once more.

As the two Guardsmen, levitating with the sling and the body between them, topped the ridge, Ethan stepped aside to give them room. Pines lined both sides of the gorge, trees like the ones in nearby Shreveport, Louisiana, the access point between his plane and the human world.

His realm had seen hard times for the past forty years and for all that time, he'd felt the weight of his realm on his shoulders, pressing down hard, just as it did on all the mastyrs, those nine vampires in charge of about a millions souls each.

Finn's phone rang. He listened for a few seconds, then brushed sweat off his forehead with the back of his sleeve. "Shit. Well, that dumb-fuck's been warned."

Ethan stared at him. "Tom again?"

Finn put his phone away. "Yep. He's at Club Prave."

"Are you fucking kidding me?" Ethan knew exactly what Tom had been up to: Violating one of Ethan's strict laws about how humans and realm-folk interact at a human-based event.

Finn grimaced. "I'll handle this."

"No. I want to this time. That asshole has been warned long enough and now I'm locking him up."

"Ethan, you've got better things to do than to police the human bars."

"Not this time. Tom Brignall hides behind his cozy relationship with Ry. Time he learned who's mastyr around here."

"He knows."

"Then why the hell is he testing my laws and my authority?"

But Finn's smile was crooked as he said, "Because he's a vampire?"

At that, Ethan almost smiled as well. But the truth was harsher. Tom had a loyalty to Ry, and had caused dozens of problems in recent years because of it.

But Ethan's other problem surfaced again, as his blood-starvation cramped him up again. He breathed through the pain wondering what the hell was going on with him. He'd never been quite this desperate where his blood-needs were concerned. And now, because of Tom's breaking of the non-tapping law at human clubs, he wouldn't have time to stop by his donor. But he'd make this quick, afterward get his blood craving slaked, or at least moved from critical to just slightly desperate, then jump back in the field.

He left orders for Paul's body to be taken to the morgue along with word that he'd check in to learn cause of death.

Before any of the men could so much as exchange a glance, or to complain again that he regularly took too much on his own shoulders, he headed south to Shreveport, levitating and flying quickly just a foot or so above the ground. He might have heard Finn grunting his frustration as he took off and he half-suspected Finn would find some excuse to follow in his wake.

Gerrod, the Mastyr of Merhaine Realm, had tried to warn Ethan that he needed to listen to his men more, to trust them more, but he was used to doing things his own way and his way was working just fine. So far, he'd kept the Invictus in check in Bergisson, and to-date, he had one of the lowest occurrence rates in all the Nine Realms.

Of course, reducing lost lives to a *tolerable statistic,* grated his nerves. There shouldn't be any Invictus left to battle, but from the time the fighting pairs had come into existence several hundred years ago, there had simply been no way, at least not yet, for his world to get rid of them permanently. Some force resided behind the Invictus, maybe the same magic that had blocked the stream at Sweet Gorge. Mastyr Gerrod believed a vampire, known to the Invictus as the Great Mastyr, and bonded with a powerful ancient fae, was experimenting with the wraith-fighting-pairs, intent on some unknown long-term goal for the future of the Nine Realms.

But where either of these entities had come from, if they even existed, Ethan didn't know, nor did any of the other realm rulers. Maybe this ancient fae had dammed up the waterfall and the stream, maybe she hadn't.

He just had a terrible feeling that if he loosened his hold even a little, his Realm would see losses like never before.

*** *** ***

Club Prave gave Samantha Favreau the creeps. From the time she'd arrived two hour ago, one vampire after another had leered at her, asking her to dance, especially the slow-dances.

She'd refused, of course, since in her opinion, vampires were just above slugs in terms of real earthly value.

But that was the point. They weren't human. They were from a different plane entirely, one somehow attached to earth.

From the time the world of the Nine Realms had made itself known to the citizenry of mortal earth, and started opening up these border clubs, more and more humans had become acquainted with what were called generally *realm-folk.*

She wouldn't be here at all, but her sociology professor had suggested using the club as a basis for one of her papers this year. He'd also upped the stakes by giving double points for studying, then writing about any aspect of the realm-world so long as the research included at least three interviews with any of the species of Bergisson Realm.

She'd already interviewed a fae female and a male troll. She was hoping one of the elves would show up. She really didn't want to talk to a vampire and the shifters in particular seemed very aggressive. Two had been thrown out already this evening for improper display of fur on the premises.

At least the club had rules, which apparently needed enforcing constantly. For instance, there was no blood-sucking allowed, but one of her classmates, Mary, had happily agreed to donate and was doing so across the room.

Samantha could see her seated on a vampire's lap, just barely visible through the throng of dancers from Samantha's vantage point. His name was Tom.

She shook her head.

Tom, the vampire.

It just didn't sound right somehow.

Leaning her back against the bar, she sipped her cosmo slowly. Her gaze shifted from one specie to the next, from the quick-footed trolls who moved like beautiful maniacs, to the lithe elves, taller than most other realm-folk, who swayed elegantly when most of the dancers jerked, twisted, and bumped, then finally to the male shifters who all looked like they could work at Chippendales.

But mostly, she avoided watching the vampires. She could at least admit she found them strangely attractive and it didn't help that most of the males were over six feet and each carried a lethal air.

From her studies, she knew the basic structure of Bergisson, that a Mastyr Vampire ruled the realm, though each of the towns and hamlets were incorporated and had governing councils. She also knew about the enemy, the Invictus, which never travelled past the access points, at least not that she'd ever heard of.

The Mastyr of Bergisson, therefore, had built up a Guard of over three hundred vampires and as she glanced at the several inching closer to her one-by-one at the bar, she'd bet each was a Guardsman. She didn't think any of them were under six-three.

She could feel their eyes on her and she could sense their hunger as though their well-known craving for blood became a kind of vibration in her bones.

She huffed a sigh, scoping out where she could go next to get away from the leeches. At least she didn't feel in any immediate danger. The owner of the club had a staff of shifters who were quite happy to tangle with the vampires and throw them out if they misbehaved.

For that reason, she knew it was only a matter of time before Tom-the-Vampire and her classmate, Mary, got in serious trouble.

The music blared, couples bounced up and down, strobes flashed. A shifter walked by, his fingers turning furry then returning to normal a couple of times as his human date squealed her excitement over this absurd trick.

She rolled her eyes.

One more male just looking to get laid.

She turned once more toward the dark corner where she could just see Mary's white thighs above her black boots, her butt cheeks almost showing beneath a short red skirt.

Sitting sideways on the vampire's lap, Mary wasn't exactly having sex, but giving up a vein to a pair of fangs was about as close as you could get. Her body moved in a back and forth, slow seductive rhythm, as the vampire sucked steadily.

The movement, very familiar in a sexual way, reminded her just how long it had been since she'd been with a man, been in a relationship, even been interested for that matter. Sometimes she wondered if there was something wrong with her, that she couldn't seem to sustain a long-term relationship with a man.

But as she watched the couples getting to know each other and all the touching, the excitement of dating, she realized part of her would be okay with a one-night anything.

Just not with a vampire.

She released yet another sigh. Okay, so she missed sex, but this wasn't exactly her idea of a pick-up bar. On the other hand, maybe she'd start making an effort to date again, if only she wasn't so easily bored with the men she usually went out with.

Samantha scowled into her drink.

The movements in the corner became more pronounced and this time, more was showing than Mary's skin. Tom's hand now pushed into one of her butt-cheeks. Donating in public anywhere in Shreveport was strictly forbidden. But what else could she expect from realm-folk at a low-life club like this one?

"Come here often?" The vampire to her left finally made his move.

Samantha's scowl deepened. Had she really just heard those words?

She couldn't help herself. Laughing, she turned and met the vampire's gaze straight on. "You gotta be kidding me? Can't men, despite the species, invent a better line than, *Come here often?*"

But the vampire wasn't in the least deterred. He blinked a couple of times and his nostrils flared. "Sweet Goddess, but you smell good." His chin quivered.

Samantha didn't like the way a pinkish sheen came over his eyes as he shifted his shoulders in her direction, licking his lips.

She thought of Little Red Riding Hood and other warning tales from childhood.

She tried to move to her right, just to get out of range, but she bumped into another vampire, this one in jeans with lots of chains attached. His nostrils worked like bellows, which really freaked her out.

Did human women smell different from vampire females?

She pushed away from the bar and felt a hand on each arm apparently intent on stopping her, but just as quickly, the same fingers fell away, which was a good thing, because she would be all too happy to start shouting for the club's owner.

She turned to glare at each of the men, but found that neither was looking at her. Something else had caught their attention and each now scanned the crowd at the front entrance to the club.

The music stopped abruptly and to Samantha's great surprise the entire club fell silent.

She had no idea what was going on until a deep, booming voice filled the air. "Where are you, Tom Brignall. I'll have your head for this."

Samantha stood very still as she watched the crowd part, realm-folk moving back swiftly, dragging surprised human partners with them, until the new arrival came into view.

A vampire.

A big one, with wild, honey-brown hair, long and somewhat curly, that flowed away from his face, most of it trapped behind in what she knew to be a woven clasp that a lot of the Bergisson Guard wore.

Then time slowed to a halt.

She blinked as a tremor ran through her head-to-foot. She'd never seen a man like this before. He had to be six-five and built, with shoulders that went on and on. He wore a traditional Guard uniform, similar to the outfit Mary's vampire wore, a black leather look that seemed to loosen Samantha's knees.

As he moved past her, she caught a scent, something wild and pungent, almost erotic, yet tough, like it grew on rocky hillsides. She shook her head, trying to clear her head because the vampire's scent was doing something to her, affecting her ability to reason, and warming things down low.

She felt a profound and quite irrational instinct to follow after him and shove her hair away from her neck.

She realized that her heart had started to pound, hard and heavy until even her throat ached.

She reached back for the bar to steady herself.

Then strangely, her vision shifted as the strobes softened and the light rose so that she saw him as if in late afternoon light, the kind when the shadows were long and the air golden. But how was it possible she could see him like this?

Right now, though, she didn't care.

He was a beautiful man, yes that was the word that came to her. *Beautiful.*

He had a soft indentation at his chin, high cheekbones, straight eyebrows that sat in a scowl over his brow. His eyes were smoky brown, like gray and light brown combined.

The uniform, she decided, was sexy as hell with leather boots that climbed his thighs and silver buckles down the sides. He wore a soft woven maroon shirt beneath a leather, sleeveless coat.

But it was his hair that struck some strange deep chord inside her, a long curled mass, pulled back by the clasp but hanging almost to his waist. She knew the Guardsmen in particular wore their hair long, a signal maybe to their enemies about their military status in the Bergisson Realm.

Her gaze slipped past him to the realm-folk who watched him sweep by. What she saw startled her because most of them appeared to be in awe, while a few low-lifes were downright scared shitless, and some of the fae women held deep lust in their eyes.

Samantha knew she must have looked like that as well, hungry for the man, a reminder that she'd been alone way too long.

She forced herself to look away from him as he headed to the far wall, setting her cosmo on the bar behind her with trembling fingers.

She drew a couple of deep breaths then heard Mary crying out, "What are you doing to him? Stop it. Oh. Oh, Mastyr Ethan, I'm...I'm sorry, but what did he do wrong?" Mary wasn't the brightest woman around.

Mastyr Ethan had come to Club Prave? The ruler of Bergisson Realm? What did this mean?

As quickly as Ethan had disappeared into the crowd, he returned hauling his prey by the thick collar of the Guardsman's coat. The vampire looked wobbly from feeding, his eyes sunken, his fangs glistening red. "Ry won't stand for this."

"You know the rules."

"Ethan, we've got him." Another male voice sounded through the club.

Samantha turned to her right, in the direction of the entrance, and at least six Guardsmen created a new flurry of excitement as they marched in.

They were an amazing presence in matching uniforms and had the females in the club panting. The foremost, with shocking red hair, hurried forward and grabbed the prisoner by the arm.

"Finn, what are you doing here?" Mastyr Ethan asked.

"Just thought we'd drop by, scope the scene." His voice held a teasing note.

Ethan didn't seem pleased, however, but Samantha had no idea why. "All right. You can take care of him, but I want him locked up for this." He then flung Tom in the redhead's direction, the one called Finn, sending the offender sprawling. The Guardsman picked him up off the dance floor. Another of the Guard grabbed his other arm and without missing a beat, they hauled him back to the entrance, then outside.

Ethan, now opposite Samantha, appeared ready to leave as well. He even stepped forward then stopped dead in his tracks.

His nostrils flared, just as the vampires had done on either side of her just a few moments ago.

She felt uneasy suddenly, like she was walking the railroads tracks and she could feel the vibrations of a train coming right under her feet but she couldn't seem to move to safety.

She also became painfully aware that her heart still pounded as she watched Ethan, and not out of fear or even desire, but out of a need to give him her most essential life-force.

What the hell was happening to her?

*** *** ***

Ethan smelled the woman first, a scent like crushed raspberries mixed with wine, like something he could lick with his tongue and savor for a lifetime.

He had meant to follow right after Finn and the other men, but the scent stopped him. Beneath that fruit-laden aphrodisiac, he caught another layer of scent: The woman's blood, and it was like nothing he'd ever smelled before, like she had rivers of it and it was meant for him.

That one thought, *rivers of blood meant for him*, made him turn toward her and stare hard.

A recent memory surfaced, of Mastyr Gerrod, a fellow mastyr vampire, who had been ready to tear Ethan to shreds for touching a woman like this one, a woman with *rivers of blood*, a woman in his realm-world known as *a blood rose*.

Gerrod had met a human named Abigail, who had relieved him forever of his blood starvation.

Sweet Goddess of Life, the woman standing alone at the bar, with vampires moving away from her on either side of her, was a goddamn blood rose.

His stomach cramped hard in anticipation of taking from her.

She must have registered his desire because she lifted her hand and pressed it against her neck as though trying to hold her vein steady. He could feel her blood singing for him, a soft vibration that forced another cramp through his stomach.

She shook her head and he could see she was bewildered. She had no idea what she was or why he, and every other vampire in the place, leered at her.

He knew the crowd was still there, waiting on him. The moment he'd entered the club, the owner had cut the music. Yet for a long, terrible moment all he could do was stare.

The woman was tall. He liked that. Shapely. Nice breasts. She wore her thick black hair straight and to the shoulders with a slight upward curve at the ends. Her eyes were the lightest blue he'd ever seen, almost unearthly. She wore jeans and a short-sleeved purple blouse, nothing fancy or even welcoming. He could smell her sex, though, her desire for him; she couldn't disguise what she felt, what she was experiencing.

Sweet Goddess, a blood rose in Shreveport, right next door to the Bergisson plane.

He walked toward her but only because he couldn't seem to help himself even though he could see from the way she wrinkled her nose that she wasn't exactly happy about what was happening.

Well, he wasn't either.

Maybe Mastyr Gerrod of Merhaine had found bliss with his blood rose, but Ethan wasn't interested in this kind of liaison. He'd watched Gerrod become possessive and lose himself in the woman, the last thing he wanted to do with any woman, human or otherwise, yet still he moved toward her.

"What's your name?" he called out.

She glanced around, growing more uncomfortable by the second. Everyone in the place stared at them both. He was used to that kind of attention; being in charge of an entire realm did that to a man, but she looked ready to run away.

Then she got mad. He saw it in the glint in her eye as she lifted her chin. "Samantha Favreau. And you're Mastyr Ethan."

"I am."

"What do you want here?"

"What do I want?" His voice boomed once more. He glared at her now, angry that her body offered what he was unwilling to take, yet something he hungered for.

He was about to force himself to turn on his heel and leave her the hell alone, when he saw something in her eye, not just a flash of anger, but this time a flash he'd often seen in the eyes of powerful fae women as they slipped into a vision.

Holy fuck, the woman wasn't just human, she was part fae.

And he'd bet his last Goddess be-damned farthing that she didn't know, or hadn't known until this very second, that she carried realm-blood in her human veins.

*** *** ***

Samantha reached to either side of her and grabbed hold of the bar, anchoring herself. She didn't understand the sensations that now poured over her, a strange vibration accompanied by images that began commanding her mind.

An entire scene came to life as though she was watching a movie, the colors rich and vivid. An event was taking place at night, a kind of fair, she supposed, with tables laden with food, trinkets, musical instruments, stuffed animals, the usual kind of carnival-ware.

At one end of a wide, playing field, lively, round canvas tents lined the grounds. They were painted with all kinds of pictures, some of woodland settings, some of animals, some of children playing games.

The vision caused her to pan to the right and over to a distant hillside, up which a beech-wood climbed to the top. But the trees grew red with what looked like fire at first, but couldn't have been since the foliage didn't catch and burn.

No, the red seemed to be a kind of wind and then she remembered from her studies that when the enemy attacked, the wraith-pairs called the Invictus, a kind of red aura would appear, followed by the fighting pairs.

As though she stood in the middle of everything, Guardsmen suddenly flew past her in their strange levitated-flight, some high in the air, others just a foot above the ground, Mastyr Ethan in the lead. On they raced in the direction of the hill, the trees, and the red wind.

The vision took her with Ethan, something that made sense since his appearance in front of her at the prave had set the strange vision off in the first place.

She watched the men, maybe fifty of them altogether, join in battle though she stayed back, yet found herself levitating high in the air. Her gaze was drawn to whatever place Ethan seemed to be as he moved up and down the line.

Pairs of strange beings, joined in some mystical, powerful way, appeared in the red wind. Jolts, like an electrical force, moved from the pairs to each individual Guardsman. A light show emerged of red and blue sparks and streams of energy, from one side to the other, back and forth.

Daggers and other weapons emerged as well, thrown, sometimes connecting. At intervals, Guardsmen rushed the pairs and brought them down screaming.

The Invictus.

She knew what made up the battling pairs: a wraith and some other enslaved realm-folk. She'd even heard that sometimes humans could engage in the same way, which made her shudder. Other than being bitten by a vampire, she couldn't think of a worse fate.

The vision suddenly tunneled down to Ethan. She could sense him faltering as he called out for Finn, his second-in-command. She could feel their bond, that they'd been brother-warriors for decades.

Finn took charge as Ethan fell to the ground.

She hovered over him now, within the body of the vision. She felt how weak he was and that it had to do with a lack of blood. Mary had told her about the mastyr vampires, those men of stature in the world of the Nine Realms who served as leaders. Something about their natural power used up donated blood at light-speed so that they constantly needed their supplies replenished but were never really satisfied.

Yes, another shudder.

She drew closer and felt herself moved to offer up her vein, because she could feel that he was close to death. Once more, her heart pounded and she touched her neck.

"He's dying. By the Goddess, we need help here. Mastyr Ethan is dying!" Finn's panicked voice rose above the sounds of the battle.

In the vision, Ethan's eyes closed. His skin paled out. Somehow, from deep within her mind, she heard him call to her, *Help me, Samantha. Only you can save me. You're a blood rose and you can help me.*

Samantha struggled to leave the confines of the vision, but Ethan was so desperate. She felt, she knew, she held his life in her hands because she was something called 'a blood rose'.

She placed her wrist over his mouth.

She heard him groan.

She saw his fangs and felt him clutch at her wrist holding her fast.

Maybe it was the force of his touch or that she could feel those sharp fangs penetrate her skin, but she somehow wrested herself from the powerful hold of the vision. She held both hands up as though warding something or someone off.

Slowly, the club came back into view, still silent.

Ethan stood in front of her, just a few feet away, but he was blurred as though the strange vision had affected her eyesight. She breathed in heavy gulps and dizziness threatened to pull her to her knees.

She heard Ethan saying something like 'back off' or 'get back', she wasn't sure. Even her hearing needed to catch up with the present.

She blinked several times and finally he came into focus. Her heart once more thudded and she found it hard to breathe. He was the one she wanted, had always wanted, would desire until the day she died.

A vampire.

Ethan.

Mastyr Ethan.

The remnants of the vision drifted away. A calmness came over her. He held her gaze steadily, looking both worried and angry, almost outraged as though she'd done something wrong.

But what had she done? What the hell had just happened to her? What was it she'd seen? Was this something that would soon happen and if it was, what responsibility did she have in this situation?

Her chest ached and she planted a fist against her sternum and rubbed. In the vision, he'd called her 'a blood rose'. What did that mean and was this why her heart beat so hard in her chest?

Ethan's gaze fell to that fist and he shook his head back and forth as though he couldn't help himself.

My God, did the vampire actually expect her to donate? Was that what it meant to be a blood rose? Well, if it did, he'd be waiting a really long time.

"I need to go home." She pressed her lips into a resolute line making sure he understood her intention, despite the fact that something so outrageous had just happened.

His lips parted and he swallowed hard. He dipped his chin and looked away from her. "Yes. You should definitely leave and it would be best if you didn't come back."

"Wait, I don't intend to return, but why would you say that?"

He lowered his chin. "Because I won't be responsible for what happens to you next time."

Her temper flared. "You weren't responsible *this* time, Mastyr Ethan. I can take care of myself."

His gaze shifted back to her and an odd light flitted through his eye, something close to respect. "Fine. Then come back as often as you like."

"I will."

He glanced around, his hard gaze landing on one male vampire after another. He watched as each faded into the crowd, never again looking at her yet at the same time avoiding Ethan's glare.

She wasn't sure, but she sensed a wave of possessiveness flow in her direction from Ethan, as though in some realm-like way, he'd staked his claim on her, warning other vampires to keep their distance.

In one sense, that wasn't a bad idea since vampires gave her the creeps in the first place. But in another sense, the same possessiveness clung to her like a velvet cloak, and against all instinct, she wanted more.

If he glared, she returned his expression in full, which made her think that he didn't like the situation any more than she did.

She said nothing more, but turned and headed back through the crowd, toward the entrance. Time to head home.

But had she actually had some kind of vision, a foreshadowing of the future? How the hell was that possible?

*** *** ***

Ethan watched the woman move in the pathway that led through the crowd all the way to the front door. She held her head high, but he sensed the depth of her confusion. She didn't know what she was and no doubt she'd never had a vision before.

He'd wanted to detain her, to talk to her, even to offer some sort of reassurance that she wasn't out of her mind, but some instinct held him back, a serious warning that the woman was trouble on all fronts.

Sweet Goddess, a blood rose in Shreveport.

Despite knowing that none of the realm-folk would return to their fun until he'd given permission, all he seemed capable of doing was watching her walk out of the building.

Then, with the disappearance of his blood rose, his current need for blood roared back to life and he listed on his feet. Nausea swept over him and he gasped. A female vampire came up to him, one of his *doneuses*, thank the Goddess.

"Mastyr?" she asked quietly.

He nodded and took her by the elbow.

She knew the drill. She stepped up on his left foot, with her left foot, slid her arm around his neck, and the crowd made an even bigger pathway.

He flew her swiftly from the building rising higher into the air to breach the cars in the parking lot.

As he did, he felt a call on him, down and to the left. As he flew forward, he glanced into the dark parking lot below, and as his vampire vision warmed, he saw Samantha turn and look up at him, her eyes wide with astonishment. Maybe she didn't frequent the prave so she probably hadn't seen a vampire in flight before, or maybe not flying quite this high.

At the same time, his personal frequency vibrated and her thoughts were suddenly in his mind. *That should be me. I should be feeding Ethan. Oh, what the hell am I thinking? What's wrong with me?*

So, she was capable of pathing, of telepathic communication. She probably didn't know that either, but it was one more indication the woman had fae blood.

He shut down the accompanying flow of frustration and disbelief. His power was ebbing and thank the Goddess that the tree-line wasn't far away.

As soon as he reached the first row of pines, he descended swiftly, the woman hopped off his booted foot, pulled her hair to the side and he was on her, his fangs nipping quickly, setting the blood to flowing. As he sucked down what was so necessary to him, but which he knew would barely satisfy his needs, his thoughts turned to Samantha, and he sucked harder, groaning against the woman's neck.

After a minute, however, of being lost in the dream of drinking from Samantha, he realized his *doneuse* was pushing against him.

He drew back appalled to see tears in her eyes. "Anita, I'm so sorry."

"It was just…rough. Mastyr, are you all right?"

Shit, because he'd been thinking about the blood rose, he'd gotten carried away. "Who the hell cares if I'm all right? Are *you* okay?"

"I'm fine." She rubbed her neck and as his vision warmed again, he saw the bruising.

"Sweet Goddess, I'm so sorry. A thousand apologies. Do you want me to summon one of the fae healers?"

But at that, she smiled. "No. I'll be fine in an hour or so, I was just surprised. You've never been like that before. Was it the woman, the human?"

He waited for her to say more, to mention that Samantha had fallen into a vision, but she didn't say anything. And he really didn't want to reveal the truth to her. "No, I was stupid. I let my blood starvation reach a critical level."

"Stupid is right when you know we're all here to serve you."

"I know that." His *doneuses* were a real blessing in his life. Early on he'd used them as much for sex as for blood, but the combination had caused too many bonding issues so that in recent decades he had a non-involvement policy with the women who donated. "How's your mother?"

"She's fine. One of the fae healers gave her a poultice and the ulcers on her legs went away within a week."

"Good, I'm glad to hear it. Do you want to go back to the prave? I'll take you back if you like."

"No, that's okay." She chuckled softly and once more rubbed her neck. "I think for now I'd better head home."

"Oh, Goddess, I'm sorry."

"Stuff it, Ethan. You're a good guy. We all think so and you're allowed to make a mistake now and then."

With that, she headed north, away from Shreveport and toward Bergisson. He turned and glanced through the trees, noting that his Guard had returned and now hovered above the ground at the edge of the parking lot, waiting for him.

Time to go kick some Invictus ass.

But as he sped in their direction, he wavered slightly and almost tipped into the pavement which would have sent him crashing into a nearby Ford truck. At the last second, he righted himself.

Well, that had never happened before.

As he landed close to his Guard, Finn called out, "What the hell was that?"

"I think I took the draw too quick."

A chuckle went through the men. What vampire hadn't been a little tipsy after slaking a blood-thirst too fast?

Of course the trouble was, Ethan knew that wasn't the real problem at all.

The real problem was that his blood rose had arrived in a half-human woman who didn't know she was part fae, and whose blood would finally ease his starvation, but for many reasons she was off-limits.

When he'd handed out orders for the next few hours, he took Finn aside and told him about Samantha. He needed at least one other person in on his current conundrum.

"What do you plan to do?" Finn kept his voice quiet. "I mean, will you take her on since she could resolve the starvation?"

"That she could take care of my blood-needs permanently is the only part of the equation that tempts me. The rest has the appearance of a nightmare waiting to happen. I felt her power, Finn, she's on Vojalie's level, or if not hers then some of the more powerful fae in the Bergisson Guild."

Finn whistled. "And she has no idea."

"Well, she does now, but she seemed pretty shocked when she left here."

Finn's phone rang, one of the Guard lieutenants informing him of an Invictus-pair sighting not far from Caldwell in the northwest, about thirty miles from the realm's wastelands. "Are you coming with?"

Ethan frowned. For one of the few times in his career, he didn't have a quick answer. Something about Samantha held him back. He shook his head. "I think I need to sort things out here first. You get the Guard on this, but if you need me, call right away. In the meantime, give me updates."

"You know I will."

As he watched Finn, and the rest of the Guard take to the air, he felt the familiar pull to be with them, his brothers in arms, to be fighting alongside them, which only made him resent even more that Samantha existed.

What a fucking mess.

Chapter Two

As Samantha drove home, she kept shaking her head like she needed to clear her ears of water. What she'd learned tonight had set her on her heels and she could hardly make sense of it all. On some level, she felt like she moved through a dream and that maybe the events at the prave had never really happened.

She hadn't imagined the vision, though, because it existed inside her now like a living, breathing thing. She could feel the images moving near the edges of her mind and that if she wanted, she could experience the whole thing all over again.

She knew from her studies of the realm-world that very powerful fae women were known to have visions. She stopped at a stoplight, watched it turn green but only stepped on the gas when the car behind her honked.

She needed to pay better attention to the road.

She kept her thoughts simpler.

She'd had a vision; she wouldn't deny the truth.

But something else became clear as she turned down her street: The vision was fae.

She'd had a fae vision.

Which meant…

She was part fae.

And the fae part of her dominated the human part.

Pulling into her driveway, she sat in her car for several long, astonished minutes.

Part fae?

But how could that be?

She got of the car and turned to stare up at a clear sky with a full moon. The April Louisiana night air was soft on her skin, not cloying like it would become in just a few more weeks.

The hour had to be past midnight.

Time even felt different to her now. She knew the hour and the minute: 12:11.

She pulled out her cell: 12:11.

How did she know the time like that?

She shook her head yet again as she made her way to the front door of what was once her beloved grandmother's home, now hers. She loved the small old house, built a long time ago. It grew into its creaking floors and musty smell, all familiar like songs that had been sung but kept echoing down each hall.

Fae.

And a blood rose.

Her heart seemed to lumber in her chest now, and when she touched her neck, the vein rose. She could feel it beneath her skin, rising for what? As though she didn't know. Rising for a sharp pair of fangs that belonged to a vampire.

A specific vampire.

A mastyr vampire, powerful, built, gorgeous, and weighed down with responsibility.

That's what she felt when she thought of Mastyr Ethan, that he bore the weight of Bergisson Realm like a stone strapped to his back.

The moment images of him moved through her mind, however, her heart began to beat really hard, like nothing she'd ever known before. She dismissed the thought that she might be having a heart attack since her newly discovered faeness knew better. A need swept over her, to reach out to Ethan, to leave her house, to enter Bergisson, to find him and to feed him, just like in the vision, to offer up her blood as his blood rose.

At the same time, she resented that she had these thoughts at all. She'd grown up knowing about the Nine Realms, and that one of them actually had an access point in her home town of Shreveport. But the most she'd ever felt about realm-folk was a sense of uneasiness she couldn't explain.

Now she knew why.

She was one of them.

She made her way to the workshop at the back of her house, where she designed her jewelry. Though she had a bachelor's in sociology and she was working toward her masters, she made her living through selling her creations online and in the local shops. Her grandmother, part squirrel by nature, had left her an inheritance large enough to allow her a certain amount of freedom. Despite the fact that she had no family left, she considered herself blessed because she was free to pursue her own dreams when so many others couldn't.

She sat down at the small antique oak desk that had belonged to her mother and which had been her favorite, something *her* mother had given her, one of the few keepsakes from a family Samantha knew little about.

Now she understood why her mother had refused, however gently, to talk about her family. How could she have when her parents had been fae? No, that couldn't be right. Her father was human; his Louisiana heritage went on and on. This was about her mother, but she didn't look fae. They had such pointed chins and strange ears. She'd seen her mother's ears.

The truth settled in on her in a terrible way that her mother's ears had been altered to fit her new human life.

Samantha felt ill. There were too many truths here to digest all at one time, too many new and frightening realities.

As she sat down, the ladder back chair creaked like the floors. This was the place her mother had written her journals, a bunch of them, all locked up in a black lacquer box, which she pulled in front of her.

"*What are you writing, mama?*" Samantha remembered asking her once.

Her mother, Andrea Bergisse, had smiled but even then, even when Samantha had been young, she'd seen and felt her mother's sadness.

"*Oh, child, just my life story in case you need to read it one day. But wait until you feel a call to my journals, not before.*" She'd had such a pretty Louisiana lilt.

"*What do you mean 'a call'?*"

"*Somethin' here, child.*" She'd put her hand against her chest and patted with her fingers. "*Here. It'll be like a soft vibration—a train whistle from a long ways away. You'll know. Promise me now.*"

"I promise."

Funny, that in all these years, she'd kept the box in its locked up state, as though she'd known all along that what lay inside was not something she ever wanted to know.

Yet, the time had come to look at the truth. She had a string of critical decisions to make, that much she understood, so she might as well get started. The sooner she figured things out, the sooner she could put this night behind her.

She placed her hand on top of the box, now smooth and cool beneath her fingers, except this time she felt a new sensation, a vibration, very subtle and as far away as that distant train whistle.

Then she got it. She was feeling fae magic, the same kind of vibrations she'd felt at the bar just before the vision had opened up.

Pulling out the center drawer of the desk, she removed the old and very dull brass key, then fit it into the box's slot. The moment she turned the key, and the mechanism shifted, the fae vibration sang up her arm, like a soft jolt of electricity. For a split second, she could almost feel her mama beside her, a hand on her shoulder, telling her everything would be all right.

But how could it be? Samantha's life had just been tossed high into the air and she had no idea what it would look like once it crashed back to earth.

She lifted the curved lid and there they were, each encased in a dull red leather, a full inch thick at the binding, five in all.

Samantha stared at the journals, but settled her hands in her lap. She didn't want to do this.

She had all that she'd ever wanted in her life, well almost. Except for a man and maybe children, she had a good life with a job she loved, enough money to live on, an important ongoing education, and a home that had been built by her paternal grandfather. She didn't need more than this. She didn't need these journals, or her overwhelming desire for a vampire, or the knowledge that she was half-fae.

And she especially didn't need to be something called 'a blood rose'.

She slammed the lid down on the box and for one of the few times in her life she gave herself to the sudden despair she felt and wept, for her family long gone, for a vision that haunted her, for a world she wished didn't even exist.

*** *** ***

Ethan followed in the wake of Finn and his team as they headed back toward the Bergisson plane to resume patrol duty.

But when he arrived at the checkpoint, he hesitated. Something nagged at him, refusing to let him leave the earth-plane. He hovered a foot above the ground, near the Guardsmen who controlled all the comings and goings between earth and Bergisson Realm, debating once more exactly what he should do next.

His thoughts were fixed on the woman, Samantha, a fae and a blood rose, who'd had no idea until this very evening that she was part realm. He couldn't imagine what she was going through right now.

He shook his head: *a blood rose*. In Shreveport.

He still recalled his first meeting with Mastyr Gerrod's blood rose, Abigail, and how with just a touch of her hand, a very human handshake, the woman had connected with his personal frequency, essentially his vampire mating frequency.

Even though he hadn't actually touched Samantha tonight, something similar had happened; his mating frequency had come alive like bells pealing in a town square. The vibration still lingered, a physical sensation he couldn't shake and which kept his drive toward her as strong as when he had first seen her.

That's when the reason for his hesitation fell into place.

He wasn't the only mastyr vampire in Bergisson.

Ry was one as well.

He knew from his original experience with Abigail that Samantha wouldn't just be attracted to him, but to all mastyrs. Her blood rose potential, therefore, made her extremely desirable in his world and in the same way made her equally as vulnerable to abuse.

These thoughts sent his mind into a tailspin of horror, of Samantha being pursued by other mastyrs, and not just by Ry, who he didn't trust, but by any of the mastyrs of the Nine Realms. Once it became known that another blood rose existed, how soon before Samantha became the object of serious pursuit? And some of the eastern mastyrs were known to be really wild.

If he didn't bind Samantha to him, one of the other mastyrs probably would. Ry, for instance, wouldn't hesitate to take her by force, especially if he thought it would give him dominance over Ethan.

For the past fifty years, since Ethan had replaced Ry as the Mastyr of Bergisson, a painful rivalry had ensued. Ry had grown bold in his attacks on Ethan, whether publicly or privately.

He'd always resented that Ethan had usurped him in the governance of Bergisson Realm, even though Ethan hadn't been the author of Ry's removal. Nine Realms laws dictated that the most powerful vampire in the land would rule the society. Once he'd come into his mastyr-power, the governing Sidhe Council, a deeply respected and ancient joint-council of the Nine Realms, had tested both Ry and Ethan and had found that Ethan's power surpassed Ry's by a significant degree.

Of course there had been downsides, one of which meant that his power as a mastyr vampire constantly drained him of his resources, putting him in a perpetual state of blood-starvation despite how often his list of *doneuses* serviced him. The other most significant repercussion, of course, was Ry and his fairly constant bucking of Ethan's authority.

Now, a blood rose had arrived, with the capacity to keep a mastyr vampire satisfied, and if he didn't do something, Ethan knew in his gut that Ry would make a play for Samantha and he'd do it tonight.

Ethan had no intention of binding Samantha. But he sure as hell wouldn't let Ry take her either. At the same time, the thought of any mastyr vampire getting near Samantha set off his battling frequency. So what was he supposed to do?

Sweet Goddess, the thought of binding Samantha, getting that close to her or any female, gave him the shakes. From the time that he'd buried his family, he'd promised himself that until he'd secured Bergisson in permanent peace, essentially eradicating the Invictus, he had no intention of building a long-term relationship with any woman. He fought the enemy every night of his life, striving to protect those in his care: a million realm-folk. He simply didn't have time to be a boyfriend to any woman—human, fae, or otherwise.

And the hell if he'd let the sudden and unexpected arrival of a blood rose change his commitment to his realm.

He slid his iPhone from the pocket of his battle leathers and dialed up his second-in-command. "Hey, Finn. I've rethought the Samantha situation. I'm concerned that Ry might get to her and you know what he's like, he won't believe that she would have any other purpose but to take care of him."

"Your woman needs protection."

Ethan repressed a hostile growl. "She's not *my* woman, Finn. Let's get that clear right now. But she does need protection and not just from Ry, but from all the mastyrs. The pull is strong and it's one hell of a seduction to think that a blood-rose could put an end to the kind of blood-starvation each of us endures."

"Do you want me to send a detail to watch over her?"

"No, I've got this."

"Once Ry gets wind of all that happened at the prave, he'll be out for your head and he'll want Samantha. He may come after you and with what I observed at the parking lot, you might want some back up."

Ethan's temper shot through his head that Finn would question his capacity to defend Samantha. But even as he opened his mouth to argue the point, his stomach balled up into a knot, and that same awful dizziness forced him to drop to earth, and plant his feet firm. He held his phone behind him, squeezed his eyes shut and burned up the forest with a long string of obscenities.

Of course once he opened his eyes, both access point Guards were smiling.

Turning his back to them, he brought his phone back up to his ear. He'd never really thought of Ry as much more than an annoying mosquito he had to swat now and then. "I'm not worried. Where are you now?"

"Patrolling near the training camp, but no Invictus sign. We're going to swing by Sweet Gorge once more. We'll give the area a thorough reconnaissance, and if nothing surfaces, I'll bring the patrol back to the Guard House."

"Good. Has the body been delivered to the Morgue?"

"Yes."

"And?"

"Death by Invictus, as suspected. But what else is new? And as with the others killed out there, the physician found a lingering fae magic."

"That's not a surprise, not from a body found at Sweet Gorge."

"I agree."

"All right. I'm heading back to Shreveport."

"Are you sure you don't want a team out there?"

"Hell, no. I can handle Ry."

A long pause told Ethan that Finn didn't approve of the plan, but that wasn't new either. Finn had been pressuring him a lot lately to give over some of his command to his top men. Ethan thought things worked just fine as they were.

"Fine, but if I get even a whisper that Ry's abandoned his patrol in the north, I'm heading south."

Though it irritated the hell out of Ethan, he knew Finn's plan had merit. "Fine." But he hung up.

When he pocketed his phone, he told the checkpoint Guardsmen to alert him if Mastyr Ry crossed into the human realm. After a moment's hesitation, he added, "And let Finn know as well."

"Yes, Mastyr." Their voices blended together in response.

Ethan rose into the air once more, higher and higher, pivoted, then flew in a quick arc back in the direction of Shreveport, just a few miles beyond the checkpoint.

The space between realms became a blurred blend of land, water, and sky then the pine trees emerged so that he knew he'd reached the distant outskirts of the North American city. Even though the realm world had first opened its doors to earth thirty years ago, crossing between worlds always gave him an odd thrill, the way ancient explorers must have felt in ages gone by.

His first thought involved wondering how the hell he would find Samantha, then he mentally kicked himself for not following her home in the first place.

He was about to return to the prave to find out if anyone knew where she lived, when another idea, more realm-like in nature, struck.

He slowed to a stop midair, hovering among the treetops, and focused on Samantha, the shape of her face, the beauty of her light blue eyes, the shine of her black hair, and mostly the blood rose vibe she gave off.

What came back to him was like a tether far away that reached for him and drew closer and closer until it connected with his chest. He stalled out for a moment, sliding down among the branches, then caught himself.

He lifted back into the air, startled by what he felt coming from her, the strength of her realm frequency which he was pretty sure she had no idea she possessed. But more came to him, beating at his senses: her distress, her sadness, like a single candle burning in the dark.

And he knew exactly where to find her.

He flew even higher into the air to avoid street lamps and power-lines. He passed by quiet suburbs and industrial buildings, even a train track and then he could see her house, a white bungalow with a white-picket fence. Her presence grew stronger within his knowing and once more his desire for her blood returned, his body full of hunger all over again, as though he hadn't just fed.

But he knew one thing for sure, that if he didn't stand guard, Ry would come for her and he wouldn't show restraint. He could feel, even now, the level of power that would come to him if he bound Samantha, which meant she'd been even more of a temptation to Ry.

He had no doubt that Ry would kidnap her and attempt to bind her without one thought for what she wanted. Most realm-bindings required an act of will to complete. Samantha would have to agree and from what he'd seen, she'd put up a fight.

But Ry was powerful and if he held her captive, he could wear her down by sheer physical torture, something he really wished he didn't believe Ry would do, but he'd had his doubts about the vampire for a long time.

And he had no intention of letting Samantha find out personally exactly what Ry was made of.

When he arrived at her house, he dropped down to earth, landing quietly outside her front door where a porch light burned. He stepped away from the house and from a reinforced pocket of his battle leathers, he withdrew a dagger.

He walked the entire circumference of her home, setting up a cloak to keep himself quiet and invisible from her neighbors. Despite this intrinsically vampire state, that he could hide himself from humans, he was pretty sure Samantha would sense he was here.

When he reached the front door again, she stood on the threshold, just behind the screen door, her lips compressed. "What the hell are you doing here and why are you tramping around like an elephant in a field of very dry grass?"

Yep, the woman was more realm than she knew.

*** *** ***

"I'm not."

"You're not what?" Samantha stared at the vampire she'd truly hoped never to see again, but here he was, in all his enormous glory, a sheen of perspiration on his forehead because he'd been flying and marching around her house for who the hell knew why. The tears had finally stopped and she'd just been working up her courage to start reading the journals, when she heard him moving near her back workroom.

"I'm not 'tramping around' as you put it; your hearing is improving. But let me assure you that right now, none of your neighbors can see me."

She glanced around. "Great. Then I probably look like I'm insane standing here speaking to you. But what are you doing at my house? I don't understand because I don't remember inviting you to come here and I must say I resent you being here."

"I wouldn't have come, Samantha, but you're in danger."

Samantha tilted her head. She knew the meaning of the words he'd just spoken, but because of all that she'd been through, the sense of what he was saying didn't register. "What do you mean I'm in danger? From you?"

He shook his head. "No, of course not. I'd never infringe on your freedoms or anything else. But there's one who might, who probably will."

"And who might that be?" The words came out drawled and disbelieving, more Louisiana than nighttime national news, but she was a little bit pissed off right now.

"His name is Ry. Mastyr Ry. He was the mastyr of Bergisson Realm before me."

She connected the dots, especially since his lips had formed a grim line. "You replaced him."

He met her gaze dead on, but remained silent.

"Oh, I see. You supplanted him. He was the ruler, then you took over."

He shook his head. "It's not done that way. The Sidhe Council tests every vampire who achieves mastyr status, and the most powerful born into each realm is obligated to rule. It's that simple."

"I'm sure this Ry vampire sees it that way."

"Let's just say that your arrival in our world will be spreading around the gossip trails like a spring flood. And Ry will want you."

Samantha took a deep breath. "And you really think I'm in danger from him?"

"Yes, because you're a blood rose."

She looked away from him. "I saw it in the vision. You were there. You called me a blood rose." Looking back at him, she asked, "But why does that endanger me?

"This gift you have, it's incredibly *tempting*, and Ry will want to possess your blood rose abilities more than anything else in the world."

Samantha blinked a couple of times. "Why didn't you tell me this back at the prave?"

"I was too caught up in your sudden arrival in my world. I didn't think about it until I was halfway back to Bergisson."

"And you honestly think he'll come here?"

"I know he will, the moment he hears about you. And that won't be long, gossip being as fruitful in my realm as it is here in yours."

Samantha shook her head. More stuff to digest. "But, even if he does come here, he has no rights. He can't do anything to me."

"I wish I could say that was true, but it's not. He'd take you illegally and only a complaint from your world could bring you back. Do you have kin who can support you? Make such a demand?"

And here was the hardest truth of all. "I have no one."

"Shit."

"Yes. Exactly. Oh, God, and I didn't think this night could get worse."

"I'm sorry, Samantha. I really am. And I'll see what I can do to ensure that he stays away from you."

"There's something else, though, isn't there?"

More grimness. "It's not just Ry. Your blood rose gift will attract any and all mastyrs, from all the realms. Once the word gets out..." He let the words hang.

Samantha understood, she just couldn't believe this was happening to her. "So, I'm a blood rose. What the hell is that, anyway?"

"It's something that's just emerged in our world. It happened to Mastyr Gerrod of Merhaine not long ago and his blood rose was a human."

"Really, as in one-hundred-percent human?" She was stunned.

"Yes, but she's now one-hundred-percent vampire."

"So, he changed her."

"More like she embraced what could be hers."

"Do I actually have the capacity to become a vampire?"

"I have no idea. I'm guessing not because you're half-fae. In our world, the species, though they intermarry, generally fall to one side or the other; the genes just line up that way." He paused, then added, "And you do understand now, that you're part-fae?"

She nodded, but her head swam with so much information. "The vision alerted me. I've been studying your world at university so I know about fae and visions, but it's still so hard to take in."

"When you're ready, you can speak with one of our fae leaders, even Vojalie, who is the most powerful fae in the Nine Realms. For now, though, can you tell me who your mother was? I mean, she was probably long-lived. I might even have known her."

"Andrea. My mother's name was Andrea Bergisse. Oh. I see." She even laughed, though she wasn't amused. "Bergisson. I just never made the connection before."

But Ethan stared at her like he'd seen a ghost. In fact, he seemed angry.

She took a step back from the screen door as she searched his eyes. "Ethan, what is it? What did I say?"

"Andrea was your mother? There's only one fae I've ever known by that name. Did she have dark hair, a little lighter than yours?"

"Almost black and wavy."

"She wore it long to the waist."

"Yes, all the years that I knew her as my mama."

He shook his head. "Sweet Goddess, for you to be ignorant of who you are, she must not have spoken of Bergisson or her heritage at all."

"No, not even a little. Whenever I asked about your realm, she told me to look it up on the Internet if I was interested. I thought she just didn't care about the Nine Realms. It never occurred to me to read her any other way. Besides, she's been gone ten years. I was only eighteen, still too young to have pieced things together. But, why do you seem so upset? Did my mother do something to you, or what?"

He was silent for a moment, looking away from her, his gaze glancing round the yard, lifting to the dark night skies as though searching, then back to her. "It was something she didn't do, but it happened forty years ago for reasons I'll never understand."

Samantha felt divorced from whatever her mother might have failed to do so many decades ago. She hadn't even been born and Andrea had been gone for such a long time that she was more ghost than a factor in her life now.

She'd loved her mother, but there had always been something off about Andrea, disconnected maybe from life. Her father's death one year before Andrea's, had stolen the last of her mother's spirit. She'd died the following spring from pneumonia, which she'd left untreated until too late.

Her grandmother was gone now as well, which led her thoughts in a new direction.

"Ethan?" He'd turned away from her, his gaze fixed skyward again, watching for Ry, maybe.

"Yeah?" But he didn't turn to look at her.

"Do I have family in Bergisson?"

At that he glanced at her, a swift searching look then set his gaze once more into the night. "I'm certain you do."

Some part of her longed to know but more, but for now, she didn't think she could handle a more detailed accounting.

"I have no family here." The words came out like a whisper. She wasn't even sure she'd spoken them aloud.

She half expected Ethan to respond, instead, he shifted to what she could only describe as a fighting stance, bending his knees, lowering his shoulders, arms held wide. A long blade flashed beneath the porch light.

He called out. "Ry, you motherfucker, make yourself known and how the hell did you get past the access point Guardsmen?" Ethan's voice echoed through the neighborhood, but he must have disguised it because not a single dog started barking, a sure sign he'd been telling the truth about being invisible to her neighbors.

If a frog sneezed, dogs started barking.

The next second, Samantha gave a cry as another vampire dropped out of the night sky, a warrior-type almost as big as Ethan and wearing the same garb; the leather sleeveless duster over a loosely woven shirt, black leather pants, and heavy, sexy boots. He held a blade as well.

His gaze slid past Ethan's shoulder and landed on her. The porch light exposed him completely but she had a feeling that even if the light hadn't been on, she could have still seen him.

She reached up and switched it off.

Sure enough, she saw both men as in a glow. Fae night vision? Realm vision?

"I can still see you, Samantha of Shreveport. Don't think you can hide from me." Ry's voice had a tinny edge, almost desperate, and maybe he was.

"You can't have her, Ry. Not now, not ever."

"Anyone can have her. She doesn't belong to you. You're not mated. She's free game and as far as I'm concerned, I have as much right as you'll ever have. More, because I've lived a century longer. Haven't you stolen enough from me?"

"I stole nothing. You know that. And Samantha is a U.S. citizen. By law, she belongs to no one. Taking her against her will, would be kidnapping and Bergisson allows U.S. law enforcement into our realm to extradite, simple as that."

"She's a blood rose. That cancels all her U.S. rights where she's concerned."

Samantha's nostrils flared and for a sudden powerful moment, Ry's scent came to her and, worse, she liked it. She smelled a heavy spice like cloves only muskier. He was a handsome vampire, not in Ethan's blond, almost flamboyant mold but darker, more dramatic, earthier.

Her body suddenly responded, her heart beating heavily as it did for Ethan, wanting to nourish both vampires. There could be no doubt that she recognized him as a mastyr, another sure sign that she was exactly what Ethan had called her in the vision: a blood rose.

"You're feeling me," Ry said, his voice husky. "Don't hide it from me, Samantha. I know that you are. You want me."

These words, however, brought a terrible sound from Ethan's throat, something between a growl and a roar. Before she could shout a word of warning, Ethan charged Ry.

Blades flashed in the glow of her vision and a heavy vibration from the battle pulsed through her in waves that kept her heart beating hard in her chest, longing for either of the vampires, wanting them both, needing to give up her vital blood supply.

The rational human part wanted the vampires to stop fighting, but this new fae self rejoiced in the battle as each man levitated and spun, avoiding the strike of the blade, lunging in for a killing blow. Ethan rose higher, to gain an advantage, and flew down toward Ry at a blurring speed.

But at the last moment, Ry shifted away, his body and leathers forming a fan-like shape as he escaped Ethan's blade. He caught Ethan's arm and jerked, which sent Ethan into the front walkway with a terrifying thud.

Samantha cried out, but Ethan rose up off the bricks as though he'd barely felt it. Vampires were strong.

Moving fast once more, he flew almost straight up and for a split-second, she saw fear in Ry's eye, as Ethan plowed into him. Ry's blade fell to the ground and Ethan tackled Ry to her front lawn where he pinned him.

The next moment, the air was full of more warrior vampires, Ethan's Guard, all wearing the traditional leather garb, floating down to her front yard to form a half-circle around Ethan and Ry.

"Now listen to me," Ethan shouted into Ry's face. "This woman, blood rose or not, has rights both here on earth and in Bergisson. You can't take her against her will, you piece of shit. Do we understand each other?"

Ry breathed hard, probably because he had Ethan almost sitting on his chest, but he nodded.

Ethan drew himself up into the air and backward a few feet, giving Ry room. "You're no longer part of the Bergisson Guard. You're out."

Caris Roane

Ry rose slowly from the ground, levitating to face Ethan an equal distance in the air. Slowly, he unbuckled the leather cross-strap that angled over his chest and let it drop to the ground. Afterward, he let the long sleeveless coat fall as well, the trademark of all Guardsmen.

Samantha felt the seriousness of the situation like a second skin and each vampire looked like he'd been delivered a hard blow to the chest.

"We may as well be clear about one thing, Ethan." Ry moved in a few inches.

Ethan's gaze became hooded and dark. "By all means, let's be clear."

"I'll have my rule back one day, you'll see, whatever it takes." He cast a sly glance in Samantha's direction. He might even have winked, she wasn't sure.

Just as Ethan lunged for Ry once more, the latter shot into the air and disappeared north toward Bergisson.

Tension held the remaining Guard immobile for several long seconds and only the sound of the long coats flapping in the breeze disturbed the night air.

Finn broke the silence. "What a prick."

A round of laughter passed through the men.

Samantha still stood behind the closed screen door. She put a hand to her chest to see if she still breathed. Her lungs appeared to be working but her heart still thumped in hard beats against her ribcage.

Her gaze slid from the Guardsmen back to Ethan. Two mastyr vampires, and she wanted to feed them both.

What kind of curse was this?

But there was a material difference between the two men: Ry would take her at any cost while Ethan spoke of her freedom and her rights.

Of the two, she had no doubt which could be trusted.

Ethan issued another string of orders, which sent most of the Guard away, leaving two behind. The remaining Guardsmen rose into the air and made slow sweeps over the roof of her house and the perimeter of her front, side, and back yards.

Ethan once more approached the screen door, but he wore a scowl that brought his straight thick eyebrows resting just above his smoky gray-brown eyes. "You're not going to want to hear this, Samantha, but I'd like you to come to Bergisson with me. Tonight. To stay in my house." He held up both hands. "Nothing funny, but Mastyr Ry has made his position clear and right now you won't be safe in Shreveport. Will you come with?"

Samantha stared at him, eyes wide, unable to blink. Now she was supposed to uproot herself and move into his house?

She wondered if this night could get any crazier or if maybe she'd just imagined everything. She needed to know more about what was happening to her. "Step back."

He obeyed.

She pushed the screen door open and moving onto the front porch, grabbed his arm, squeezing tight. A vibration ripped through her. "What is that? What am I feeling? I need to understand some things here."

"My personal frequency. We're a world of vibrations and frequencies."

The vibrations ebbed and flowed, almost like a conversation. Then she realized some of the vibrations emanated from her. The whole experience felt wonderful, extraordinary and completely unnerving.

Ethan winced and groaned. "Oh, God, you smell like heaven, the sweetest fruit and wine together."

His eyes were shut as he licked his lips.

She couldn't be imagining this sensation, a feeling of consecutive waves passing through her, tightening her abdomen and once more causing her heart to thud and her blood to flow thickly in her veins.

"And you smell like rich earthy grasses, something that grows wild on a hillside." Her nostrils flared as he opened his eyes. "And you're real, aren't you?"

"I am." His deep baritone voice enhanced the vibrations. She released his arm, a necessary act. She was feeling too much.

She shuddered as she drew back.

Turning away from him, she let the screen door slam shut. "You want me to stay in your home in Bergisson? You, the ruler of that realm?" She thought it was akin to being offered a stay at the governor's mansion.

But at that, Ethan smiled, showing all his big beautiful teeth. "I don't bite, except on request."

"Now you're going to flirt with me?"

"Only if it takes some of the sting out of the moment. Seriously, Samantha. Ry means business."

"I can see that he does, but this is all so new, so bizarre, too much to take in."

"You're right. Of course." He frowned again, something he did a lot. "Let me put it this way. Until we get this thing sorted with Ry, you'll be safer in Bergisson than here and since it appears you've just discovered tonight that you have fae blood, I can try to make contact with Merhaine and bring Vojalie to stay at my house as well. She's a very wise woman and our most powerful fae. She'll be able to answer every question."

Some of the tension left her body. "I have to admit, that sounds much better."

He leaned forward. "She'll be able to tell you everything about who you are, even about Andrea, things I wouldn't know or have access to. She might even be able to show you around the Fae Guildhall, one of the most revered, historical buildings and organizations in our realm."

A Fae Guildhall.

"How long do you think I'd be staying?"

"I have no way of knowing, but at least until I can secure your safety. If that means hunting Ry down and putting him in prison, then that's what I'll do."

Samantha released a long, deep breath. "Could Ry bind me by force permanently if he wanted to?"

"He could wear you down, yes." Ethan ground his jaw. "But I sure as hell won't let him get that close."

Of all the men she'd ever known, she was pretty sure Ethan could make good on his words. "Let me just pack a few things."

The tension rushed out of him like a wind that passed through the screen, the sensation was that strong. "Thank you. Take all the time you need."

*** *** ***

One of the Guardsmen held Samantha's suitcase as Ethan showed her how to balance herself on his right foot for the flight home. He felt her nervousness as she slid her arm around his neck, arranging her grip carefully beneath the mass of his long, thick hair.

He held her tightly against him so that she could perch both of her much smaller feet on his right boot.

"We good?" he asked, his gaze sweeping the sky overhead. He didn't think he could bear to meet her gaze in such close proximity. As it was, his control hung by a thread.

"Yes." She even nodded and he could feel her heart beating powerfully in her chest, working to provide what he needed.

His mouth watered. Sweet Goddess did his mouth water. Her raspberry-wine scent was thick in his nose and he could smell her blood, like an elixir from heaven.

And if that wasn't enough, her body pressed against him had ignited his personal frequency and desire for her flowed once more. He'd never been more grateful for the leather coat and snug battle leathers that right now hid one major sin.

He forced himself to breathe. "I'm going to launch now, but I have you." He drew her tight against him.

"Do your worst."

He liked that she showed so much courage. She'd had to process a lifetime of change in only one night.

To his Guard, he called out, "Back to Bergisson."

The men gave a shout as they launched into the air. He followed behind in case Ry chose to attack.

He'd already warned her that if the sight of trees coming at her freaked her out, to just turn into him and close her eyes.

To the woman's credit, however, she faced forward, as much as she could with his arm like a vise around her.

"This is amazing."

"You aren't afraid?"

"Not yet, but give me time."

He smiled.

At the checkpoint, he nodded to the Guardsmen who inclined their heads in response. He pressed on, flying swiftly through the oak forest that bordered the southern lands of his realm with the northern Shreveport regions. If he continued north, his realm would open onto an expansive valley where at least a third of his population lived in the major city of Cameron.

He shifted course, however, heading east toward the wooded hills that held his main property. On the outskirts of his land was the Guard House, a home base for his troops as well as a training facility.

He heard Samantha gasp softly as he crested yet another oak laden hill, then descended toward his modern, primary residence that housed a huge, crystal embedded, glass conservatory. Large oaks on the hill behind and throughout the grounds shaded the house.

The hour was late for a human, past one in the morning, and the woods dark. "Are you able to see everything, Samantha, even though it's night?"

"Yes, there's a soft glow everywhere, as though the earth is lit up, like it's early evening, with the sun barely set. How is that possible?"

"That's realm vision so that those of us fated to remain indoors during the day can have the company of all realm-folk without massive amounts of candles or lamps. You'll find that at least half our people have a degree of sensitivity to sunlight."

"Your home is beautiful. The lines and materials are modern, yet you've used wood in big arching curves to soften the effect. The balance is perfect."

"You speak like an artist."

"I am. I design jewelry."

"Ah." As he touched down a few yards from the front door, he released her slowly. "Check your balance."

She stepped off his foot. How reluctant he was to remove his hand from her waist, to have her arm slide from his neck. Breaking the physical connection almost *hurt*.

She turned to look up at him, blinking, her lips parted. "That was so strange. The disconnection, I mean." She touched his chest, clearly without thinking, and his vibration rose to meet her as though greeting an old, familiar friend.

Her hand rested between his pecs. He didn't say a word. He didn't move. He didn't think he could. He just wanted her touching him.

His desire for her sharpened almost painfully and again he was grateful for the coat to hide what had become very stiff and full of intention. Goddess, he was a mess.

His Guard hovered in the air at least twenty feet away. He lifted his right arm slowly, raising his palm to keep them in place. He didn't want to break this moment with Samantha. He understood that she needed to experience his frequency right now, to take in the enormity of what a connection to a mastyr vampire would be like, to add to her understanding about the nature of what it was to be a blood rose.

He could feel how easily he could seduce her right now, to travel through his frequency to hers and to work her up sexually.

It would take so little. Did she know that? Did she understand how much effort it took for him to restrain himself?

Slowly, she lifted her gaze to his. "You're trembling," she whispered.

He nodded, just a brief jerk of his head. "It might be best if you took your hand away now. I won't be able to hold back much longer because I'm tempted on every level. Do you understand? The need for blood and the need for sex often come together."

She frowned slightly as she stared at her hand, but she didn't pull back.

He wondered why she hesitated, but if she didn't do it soon, he swore he wouldn't be able to answer for his conduct.

Chapter Three

Samantha knew she needed to withdraw her hand, but she didn't want to. She felt his vibration on the tips of her fingers and she felt his call on her in every pulse of his frequency, to come to him, to lie down with him, to let him take her. His vibration had tapped into something deep inside her and she loved the way it felt, especially the intense sexual component.

But this last thought, that she wanted to climb into bed with Ethan, finally brought her to her senses.

She half-slid, half-pulled her hand away from the soft leather of his coat and the stiffer band of his cross-strap. But for a long moment, she looked into his eyes and let the experience flow through her, of who he was in his world, of his frequency, of the sheer size of him.

A breeze blew down from the surrounding hills and she shivered suddenly, which put him in motion. "Let's get you inside. The night's cold for half-humans."

She chuckled at his word choice.

Half-human.

Oh, God, *half-fae.*

Was this truly who she was now? Who she always had been, but didn't know herself to be?

He turned to the vampire holding her suitcase thirty feet above and held out his arms. He meant to catch it.

Samantha wanted to protest: the bag was heavy and the vampire in the air was so far away. Gravity and acceleration combined would add force to the weight of the suitcase.

But before she could say anything, the man above dropped the case, Ethan caught it easily, then slung it over his left shoulder.

Vampires were strong.

Her heart fluttered in her chest.

He called out to his men, ordering them to the Guard House and to check in with Finn. The entire vampire escort turned east and flew farther down the hill. He explained that he had a large, nearby training camp for his Guard, which also had a rec room and a bar for the warriors to let off steam. And a huge modern house that belonged to the ruler of the realm, all steel, wood, and glass.

Once inside the house, he swept his arm to the left. "The main living areas are at this end, including the kitchen, so if you need anything to eat, day or night, please help yourself. I have staff that comes in around four in the morning, when I usually return from my patrols, so don't be surprised if you hear them, but they leave a few hours later when I head for bed.

"A cleaning crew arrives late afternoon because that's when I'm usually emerging from my cave. I'll let them know that I have a guest in residence so you won't be disturbed."

He waved his arm to the right, encompassing a short but broad staircase. "The bedrooms and a second living area are this way. You'll have a suite to yourself, of course, with a sliding glass door to the conservatory that you can open and close at will."

Samantha could see that the house was built to the contours of the land since another short staircase led down toward the living room and a massive stone fireplace.

At the far end of the room, a set of three stairs led upward once more, to a dining area with a huge table and large upholstered chairs. The kitchen was hidden from view by a long, brick wall.

The furniture, in subdued browns, blacks and grays, all seemed oversized, but then Ethan, as well as the Guardsmen she'd seen, were all big men.

Beyond the glass windows, she saw extensive landscaping with shrubs, lawn, flowerbeds all leading to the hillside and a short stone wall with wide, seating pavers on top. The oaks, grasses and shrubs past the wall had been left in a natural state to grow wild.

With her case in hand, he gestured for her to ascend the stairs to the right.

At the first landing, rooms off to either side clearly belonged to Ethan's job as a mastyr. One held a desk, a computer with two screens, filing cabinets, stacks of papers and folders. The room to her right looked more like a library but had a massive table in the center onto which an old map was laid out and weighed down with beautiful split-geodes, their colorful crystals winking beneath a soft overhead light.

"You have lights on."

"By habit. My vampire vision is perfect at night, but we have several species in the Nine Realms who struggle if some lighting isn't available."

"Then it's a courtesy."

"No. A necessity. I think there's a difference."

'Splitting-hairs' came to mind.

Another short flight of stairs led to a second sitting area with another stone fireplace, smaller than the one in the living room but still impressive in size.

He tossed his arm in a quick side motion. "There are several bedroom suites here in the south wing, but I'll want you closer to my rooms for safety." He then gestured forward. "Beyond the living area is the suite you'll be staying in as well as my rooms." He guided her past a grouping of couches and chairs. "And here to the right is the conservatory. I thought you might like to see it. Most of the fae I know really enjoy this space."

He directed her to a large arched doorway opposite the fireplace.

She stood at the entrance and gasped for the breadth and height of the room, the welcome fresh air that came from hundreds of plants and trees, and the beauty of the crystal roof that peaked at least sixty feet in the air, maybe higher.

"This is huge."

"It is."

Then she felt something, a kind of singing vibration from the room, which drew her a few steps inside. "What is that?"

"What is *what*?"

"I'm feeling another kind of vibration from this room."

"You are?" He sounded surprised.

She turned and met his gaze. "Don't you feel that? Hear that?"

He seemed taken aback as he narrowed his gaze and once more glanced around the massive room. "I don't feel anything, just the air circulating."

"It's not your air conditioning. I'm sure of that. I'm hearing a kind of music."

"Some fae, when they get near crystals, can hear melodies of a kind, but it's very rare. Now that I think about it, Vojalie said she loves this room, maybe that's why."

"But she never mentioned a singing quality?"

"No, but then she'd have no reason to say anything if she experienced a fae reaction, which reminds me that I need to bring her here."

"You look troubled."

"I alluded to it earlier, but we've been having some kind of breakdown realm-to-realm in recent weeks. Sometimes it'll clear up then close again, like someone has shut a door."

"And that's not normal?"

"No, not at all."

"What do you think it is?"

He turned to her. "To say anything else right now would be irresponsible on my part. Let's just say that I'll do my best to get Vojalie here. I know she'll want to meet you and talk to you and she'll be the best person to introduce you to our world."

Samantha nodded and turned away from the door. The sensation of leaving the conservatory, however, felt like fingers drifting off her arms slowly and reluctantly. For whatever reason, she didn't want to leave.

When he showed her to her guest suite, she was bowled over by the sheer size of the space. He moved into the room and turned the light on for her, though he winced a little as he looked away.

She could have put two of her bedrooms in this one room and the bed itself had to be king-sized.

She released a deep sigh. For all the weirdness of the night, the one thing she felt right now, besides a sudden overwhelming fatigue, was that she felt safe. "Thank you, Ethan. You didn't have to do any of this for me."

He settled her bag on the upholstered bench at the foot of the bed. But he looked so surprised, with his brows high on his forehead and his lips parted, that she said, "What?"

"Of course I did. You're my guest. But I think I know what you mean." He sighed. "And I'm grateful you came with me, when you didn't have to."

"Oh, yes, I did. Ry is one sick nutcake."

At that he laughed, showing his beautiful smile and all those big white teeth of his. He was a gorgeous man, prettier than he ought to be, and he smelled wonderful, those rich hillside grasses again.

"Well, at least we agree on that." He held her gaze tight to his and there it was all over again, a need for him so profound it was like having the wind knocked out of her, but she held steady.

"Yeah, we agree on that."

She stood near the foot of the bed unable to move and her brain had stopped functioning because she really couldn't think of anything else to say.

He seemed to understand. He looked away from her and cleared his throat. "Can I get you anything?"

She shook her head. "No, thank you. I think all I need right now is some sleep."

"I'm sure you do."

He moved past her, heading to the door. He gestured to a long bank of floor-to-ceiling drapes patterned in a soft gray swirl. "The conservatory is right there. Feel free to open the sliding door if you want." He smiled again, softer this time. "Maybe the 'singing' will sweeten your dreams."

"Thanks, I might just do that."

He nodded. "Anything, Samantha. Really. Just ask." Through the open doorway, he glanced down the hall. "My rooms are the double door at the end of the hall. Shout. I'll hear you."

She dipped her chin a few times.

"Okay," he murmured, slapping the doorframe twice. He then closed the door and she heard his muffled footsteps as he headed back the way they'd come. No doubt he had more realm business to tend to.

She put a hand to her chest, however, aware of her laboring heart. "Yeah," she whispered. "I know. But try to calm down. He's just a man. I mean a vampire." Then she laughed, because it was all so strange, and horrible, yet wonderful at the same time.

She hadn't expected an adventure when she left for the prave earlier that evening, but it looked like she'd gotten one.

*** *** ***

Ethan rubbed his forehead as he moved back down the first set of stairs then headed into his office. He glanced at some notes he'd made that afternoon about realm details he needed to deal with, especially issues with some of the towns and cities. But now was not the time.

Instead, he called Finn.

"How we doin' out there?"

"Quiet. Very quiet."

Ethan could hear the concern in Finn's voice. Invictus activity made the night hard, but the lack of it wore on all the Guardsmen's nerves. A lull never meant good things, usually a serious gearing up for something big.

"Well, shit."

"Ethan, you don't think Ry would join forces with those bastards, do you?"

"I don't know. I've never really known him, just his rage because the Sidhe Council voted him out and me in."

"You're the better man and don't you forget it. There isn't a vampire on the force who won't cheer that he's gone. You can count on that. Should have been done a couple of decades ago."

"I never felt right about stepping in. This was his realm."

"I'm not going to waste time arguing with you on that score again. You're the vampire for this job."

Ethan sat in his leather chair and released a heavy sigh. "Yet I can't seem to get the better of the enemy that we've battled all these years, these decades. We dispatch hundreds of wraith-pairs every year and bury twice as many realm-folk. Does that make me the better leader?"

"It was worse under Ry. And he'd been running three illegal gambling joints as well."

"Small comfort."

"So how's your woman?"

"Not my woman, Finn, and if you want to keep your front teeth and a pair of fangs, you'll keep your trap shut."

Finn chuckled. "Just giving you grief."

"Hey, thanks for showing up tonight."

"Within a half hour of leaving you, I'd gotten word that Ry had abandoned his northern patrol."

"Well, I was glad to have witnesses for giving Ry the boot."

"It was a pretty sight, but how are those precious knuckles of yours?"

Ethan looked at his hands. He was already healed up, despite his blood-starvation. "Content."

Finn cleared his throat. "Just one suggestion, though."

"What's that?"

"Call a donor. You were looking pale when I left."

"You my mama now?"

"You know I'm right."

Ethan did know, but the thought of bringing in one of his *doneuses* with Samantha in his house felt like a kind of betrayal he couldn't easily explain. "Call me if you need me."

"Yes, mastyr."

After ending the call, Ethan sat for a good long while in his office. He took stock of his condition and he didn't like what he saw, what he felt.

Earlier, Samantha had said he was trembling. At the time, he thought her presence had brought on the strange sensation. But the truth bit deeper. His blood-starvation, always at a difficult level, had sunk to critical and the earlier donor had barely scratched the surface of his need. Sure, his mastyr status kept him in this chronic, undernourished state, but usually a feed would keep him stable for twelve, sometimes eighteen hours.

He lifted his hand off the arm of the chair.

His fingers shook.

This was new and not good.

He swiveled, angling back up the hall in the direction of Samantha's door. What he needed lay just beyond a few inches of carved, fine wood.

But he couldn't go there. He couldn't do that to her and he knew once he got started, he wouldn't be able to control himself, not with her, not with a blood rose.

And sex would follow.

Because the trembling increased, he finally understood that her presence made his symptoms worse, so he had no other choice, but to call for help. He arranged for a later feed, just before his patrols for the following evening.

For now, rest would help, so he headed back the way he'd come.

Maybe facing off with Ry had taken a toll, and clearly meeting his blood rose had hit his reserves hard, but he needed sleep. He had his cell with him and in an emergency, he had a support call service hooked up to an intercom system in his house.

He paused only once, just outside Samantha's door. He heard a soft humming sound, a single pitch, somewhat high. He suspected she was matching the sound the crystal ceiling made for her.

He shook his head, as disbelief, maybe even shock, still worked within his mind.

Once inside his rooms, he stripped and showered, then lay down on his bed. He'd fully intended to have a hard think about his current situation, but like the proverbial head-hitting-the-pillow, he was asleep and slept until his alarm sounded at four the next afternoon.

He woke up not feeling rested at all, but rather like horses had stomped on him all night. He sat up dizzy and put his head in his hands. He needed blood. Now.

Naturally, his thoughts turned to Samantha, which cramped up his stomach into a fierce knot of pain. He swore he could smell her blood even though at least forty feet of house separated them. He slid from bed and found it was easier to tolerate his condition so long as he kept moving.

All that held him together was the knowledge that his *doneuse*, Angela, would arrive soon.

He showered quickly then placed a phone call to the Merhaine Realm. He said a quick prayer that communications between Realms would be open because he needed help with Samantha, help he couldn't give her, not even a little. He was a vampire. Her faeness could only be interpreted by another fae and his choice for serving up all that information landed on the most powerful in the Nine Realms.

The phone rang and rang and just as he'd begun cursing fate, Davido answered. "Hello and good eventide to you. Vojalie the Wise's residence, your handsome troll here. With whom do I have the great pleasure of speaking?"

Ethan smiled and shook his head. Warmth spread through his chest. He had great affection for both Vojalie and Davido and often forgot that, unlike he and his Guard, most realm-folk led relatively normal lives.

Davido was old, as in no one really knew how ancient he was. He'd never, therefore, fully taken on modern speech patterns. "Ethan here. How's it hangin', my friend?"

"Ah, Ethan. How uplifting to hear your voice! What nonsense we have these days with the realm-to-realm access points coming and going like fog rolling through then disappearing only to come back. Have you Andrea's daughter there with you?"

"Wait, what? How the hell did you know that? Has someone called you tonight?"

"Nay. Tis my beautiful one. The ceiling dome of her living room has been cloudy and at times black. Imagine, *black!* Visions and headaches have settled on her and she's been weeping for Andrea again. She said Andrea's precious daughter would be in Bergisson soon. So, you have her?"

"Yes."

"And did you say anything to her, about Vojalie I mean and Andrea?"

"No, of course not. I thought Vojalie should be the one to tell Samantha about her mother and all things fae. But we need your wife here, Davido. Is there any chance—"

"She's been packed and waiting for your call these five days."

Five days. Sometimes he forgot how different the fae were from vampires. "Well, good, that's good. Can you bring her now and the baby, of course. She'll want the baby with her."

Vojalie had given birth not long ago and the fae were she-bears when it came to offspring. He wondered if Samantha would be the same, a thought that led to a sequence of images that ended with her belly full of his child and how he'd gotten her that way.

He gripped his stomach and bent over at the waist. Could a vampire perish from lust? He began to think it possible. Sweet Goddess, he needed to get fed and laid, the sooner the better.

"Of course Bernice will be with her and I shall accompany them both."

"I was hoping that would be the case. I'll have Vojalie's favorite guest suite prepared for the three of you."

When he hung up, he spent the next five minutes just breathing through the pain. He couldn't put this off. He placed a second call to hurry up the appointment and within a few minutes, his *doneuse*, Angela, walked into his bedroom, a frown between her brows.

"Ethan, why did you wait so long? You look like you haven't fed in weeks. Is it true your blood rose has come? It's been all over the Bergisson blogs."

He nodded and waved her forward. "You'd better just give me the inside of your elbow. I don't trust myself at your neck."

"Whatever you need, mastyr, you know that." Angela had a husband and three children, all in elementary school. She'd been serving him for decades and at one time had been one of his lovers, but that was years ago.

He respected her choices and never, *never*, crossed the line with any of his *doneuses* once they took a husband, regardless of species. She was a wife to a powerful shifter, a wolf named Smack, a descriptive name for exactly what would happen to Ethan if he ever strayed from his principles.

He bit quickly and struggled to keep from collapsing the vein by sucking too hard. She spoke quietly to him about her children, which helped a lot to keep him on an even keel, especially to prevent him from thinking about what existed off the conservatory, in one of his guest suites, so close, so close.

Ah, Samantha.

"Hey, easy does it, mastyr. Smack won't want to see a bruise."

He gentled his suckling and focused hard on the home run her second son had made in T-ball.

When he finished, he fell back against the bed. At least his stomach had settled down. "Thank you."

"Sweet Goddess, Ethan, you don't look much better than when I came in. I take it your blood rose hasn't given it up for you?"

She smiled when she spoke, teasing him, but the imagery made him sit up again way too fast. His head swam and he barely kept from throwing up what she'd just given him. "Don't talk like that about her." Now he was defensive. Great.

"I can see I'd better go."

"Thanks again, Angela."

"Anytime."

He waved a hand and heard her leave, the door snapping shut behind her.

How the hell was he supposed to get through the night's patrols in this condition? And what would he do if Ry chose to challenge him?

*** *** ***

At four-thirty in the afternoon, Samantha sat in Ethan's conservatory and dined on some of the finest food she'd ever eaten, made savory by the herbs grown in the mastyr's kitchen garden.

Marta, the housekeeper and a lovely troll, had set up a table in the conservatory, then brought her a perfect spinach omelet and a shallow bowl full of succulent mixed berries.

She enjoyed the black tea, in particular, sweetened as it was with raw sugar and cream.

She felt really spoiled except for the fact that she was no longer in Shreveport and that her life had been turned upside down.

Staring up at the crystal apex, the music had never been prettier. She'd awakened to it throughout her sleeping hours, aware that the sounds resonated with a part of her deep inside, the part that was fae.

Just as she set her mug on the wrought iron table in front of her, she felt a strange vibration deep in her chest, not a warning exactly, more like an announcement or a revelation.

She stood up with a hand between her breasts. Her heart still thudded around in her chest, of course. That was a given because of her proximity to Ethan.

But this felt different.

Again, this felt *very* fae.

She pivoted toward the arched doorway and there, cast in a glow from the sun still lighting up the crystal roof, stood the most beautiful woman she'd ever seen, and she was fae.

Vojalie.

Samantha felt the woman's identity in her bones, as if she'd always known her.

She was tall, like Samantha, probably close to the same height, though Samantha might have been a little taller. She had fae features, a thin nose and a chin that came to a strong fae point, though not so severe as most. She wore a narrow headband to hold back her dark brown hair, which hung past her waist ending in a series of soft curls. Her dark eyes, which twinkled, matched her hair.

"You must be Samantha even though I confess you don't look a great deal like your mother."

"I was always told I resembled my daddy. I could see it in the mirror, as well. Now that I see you, I realize how *fae* she really was."

She began walking toward Vojalie as though pulled by an ancient connection. She almost thought 'family', which she supposed came from their shared heritage as fae.

Vojalie, standing beneath a large ficus tree, held out both her hands and smiled. "I'm so glad to meet Andrea's daughter."

When Samantha reached the powerful fae, she didn't hesitate, not even for a second, to put her hands in Vojalie's.

She gasped as a sensation like a balloon flying into the air took hold of her. She felt light, buoyant, free, a strange, euphoric experience. "I feel like I'm coming home after a long absence, but how is that possible?"

Vojalie's warm brown eyes filled with tears. "I missed your mother so much. I took her death hard. We barely spoke after she moved to Shreveport so that I never even knew about you. She wanted a different life, you see, and nothing more to do with me or Bergisson or any of the Nine Realms. I had to respect her wishes so I hope you'll understand that."

"Well, of course." Samantha withdrew her hands from Vojalie's soft grasp. "But you must have been really good friends at one time. I mean you speak like you were sisters or something." Vojalie didn't look older than Samantha, but the world of the Nine Realms was a long-lived world, something she had to keep remembering.

A slight frown appeared between Vojalie's strong, arched brows as though she was trying to figure something out.

Finally, she said, "We were both those things, friends and fae-sisters, if you will. I was grief-stricken when she left our world. But she had a terrible time when her fae husband, Patrick, died. He'd been a rock in her life and that year following his death, nearly forty-one-years ago now, sent her spiraling into a dark place. I know that's when she started thinking about leaving Bergisson."

Samantha stared at Vojalie as she processed this new revelation, one of so many. At some point, when she was ready to read Andrea's journals, the five red leather tomes would undoubtedly be able to fill in a lot of the missing blanks. She'd even packed the journals in her suitcase, but didn't feel the time was right to dig in.

Now Vojalie was here, a different source of information.

"So, my mother had another husband. I never knew, but she never told me much about her life, and now I can see why since she'd had to lie about most of it. She said she'd come from New Mexico but had lived in Louisiana for the past thirty years before she died."

"I see." Vojalie seemed very distressed, her brow puckered, her expression grim. "When I spoke with Ethan earlier, I guess I forgot to ask how much you knew. All that he told me was that last night was the first you'd learned about being part-fae. I suppose I should have guessed that Andrea would have kept silent about her former life."

Marta appeared in the doorway with a fresh pot of tea and a second mug. Samantha turned and led Vojalie back to the small wrought iron table.

The lovely troll housekeeper arranged things quickly, setting out the teapot and the second mug. She brought forward an additional chair as well.

Samantha gestured for Vojalie to sit down, then resumed her seat.

Vojalie sipped her tea, the frown showing again. "So you know nothing about the realm-world."

"Only what I learned from school-ground gossip growing up, then later through university and the Internet, and last night, of course, I met Ethan at the prave."

"Do you often go to praves?"

Samantha held her mug cradled in her hands. "Never. I wanted nothing to do with your realm-world. Or I suppose I should say 'our' realm-world now, but it still feels so wrong." She glanced around the conservatory. The soft music of the crystals eased her and she almost asked Vojalie if she could hear them as well, but decided against it. "I just wanted a quiet life in my grandmother's home, making my jewelry, studying for my masters."

"And is that your dream then? Living in your grandmother's house, making jewelry, exploring your education?"

"Yes and no. I'm content with my life in Shreveport, but I guess you could say my real dream was to have a cottage by a lake, surrounded by weeping willows and more lawn than I could manage by myself. And the cottage would be made of river-rock, you know tumbled boulders."

Once again, Vojalie teared up, but she brought her mug to her lips.

"Is it something I said?"

Vojalie shook her head. "I gave birth three months ago, I'm nursing, and you remind me how much I lost when Andrea left. I'm just so overcome. She was very important to me."

"I can see that she was."

She felt dizzy suddenly as a new thought surfaced. "How old was my mother when she left Bergisson? The year she died, when

I was eighteen, I asked her age, but she laughed and said, 'twenty-nine'. It was her joke about never wanting to grow old."

"Part of that statement was true. She would have been two-hundred-and-twenty-nine at that time. If she were alive today, she'd be ten years more."

Samantha put a hand to her forehead and squeezed her eyes shut. There was just so much to take in and with Vojalie's arrival, everything she'd been hearing had become a very long stream of jolts.

"So she was that old?"

"We're long-lived."

"So you are."

"Samantha, I'm so grateful that Ethan thought to call me. You must have a thousand questions and I want you to know that I'm here for you, whatever you might need from me, anytime, anyplace. For your mother's sake alone, I would make this offer, but I'd also extend it to anyone in your circumstances, who's just found out she's part fae. So, how did you find out? I take it something specific happened."

Samantha drew in a deep breath and told her everything, from arriving at the prave, of seeing her classmate with Tom-the-Vampire, of the way the other vampires seemed to hover around her, then of Ethan's dramatic arrival.

"So Tom was there?"

"Yes. He's in jail for violating one of Ethan's laws about feeding in public in the human world."

Vojalie sipped her tea again. "Oh, Tom, yes, he's a hopeless sort." Glancing at Samantha over the rim of her mug, she added, "But Ethan's formidable-looking, isn't he?"

Samantha's thoughts shifted sideways as she recalled seeing Ethan for the first time. He'd moved with lethal grace, the stride of an athlete, of a man made for war, heavily muscled, his body toned for battle.

She'd never seen anyone like him before, vampire or human. "He's very tall," she said quietly.

"And way too handsome for his own good. Most of the mastyr vampires seem to be blessed in that way, but Ethan's got that gorgeous smile of his. I swear he radiates sunlight when he's truly amused."

"That's it." Samantha laughed as she turned to Vojalie. "I've seen that expression. I know what you mean. He sort of lights up."

She then related the events at Club Prave, how Ethan had caught her scent or felt her vibration or something, how he'd looked at her, the way she'd felt about him though she knew him only by reputation, that she'd connected with what he called his personal frequency, that her heart had become sluggish and he'd called her a blood rose.

She told her the rest as well, how Ethan had essentially protected her from Ry, insisting she have her freedom. "He asked me to come with him and I'm sure if I hadn't heard the things Ry said, I would have stayed behind at my house. But it seemed foolish not to come. Besides, I knew he'd stay outside my house all night if I didn't. Ry was determined to have me."

"I can understand why Mastyr Ry might have felt that way, though of course I don't approve. Personal freedom is very important here in Bergisson just as it is in your world. But the mastyrs truly suffer." Vojalie then spoke of the blood-starvation that all the mastyrs experienced. "It has something to do with the natural level of power each mastyr carries, including Ry, that it must use up some essential element that the average woman can't replace. I saw the change in Gerrod immediately, once he began feeding from Abigail, like he'd been taking vitamin shots round the clock."

Samantha drew in a long, deep breath. "But I didn't ask for this."

At that, Vojalie chuckled. "Get in line. Most of the time, I'm content with my lot but there are days I just wish someone else could do what I do."

"And what do you do?"

"I'm leader of the fae community in all Nine Realms and I sit on the Sidhe Council. Every significant problem relating to our fae-folk comes to me for both judgment and resolution. Some of the problems are simple and relate to an improper balance of spells, potions, and herbal concoctions. Others are much more difficult, like the interpretation of visions that relate to the Invictus. You do know about the Invictus."

"A little."

Vojalie sipped again. "Well, that's a conversation for another time. Ah, here is my husband, Davido, and our newest addition, baby Bernice." Smiling, she called out, "Davido, come meet Andrea's daughter, Samantha."

"Ah, my love, nothing would please me more. Dear, sweet, troubled Andrea." He drew close, the troll infant slumbering in his arms, a very small bundle against his chest. He wore blue plaid flannel. "How do you do, Samantha of Shreveport. I see you're admiring my shirt. I must look like an undersized lumberjack."

"Yes, maybe." Samantha grinned. There was something in Davido's expression that put her at ease. He wasn't a handsome troll, not even a little, though she knew that every realm species had a full range of what was considered handsome or beautiful all the way to homely. But something in the gleam in his eye drew her to him, a certain charisma.

She stood up, and bent her head to get a good look at the baby, just three-months-old.

"Would you like to hold her?"

Samantha drew in a sharp breath and held out her arms. Davido transferred the swaddled infant as though giving her the greatest gift on earth, or in the realm. Maybe he was. Nothing was more precious than new life, all the promise encased in one being, human or otherwise.

She got lost in the joy of holding the child and to their credit, both parents let her be.

*** *** ***

Since it was almost time to head out for patrols, Ethan knew he would do better once he left his house and Samantha behind. But as he walked through the sitting room, he could hear his guests cooing over baby Bernice, presumably from within the conservatory. He could hardly refuse to greet them.

The problem was, he saw faint spots at the edges of his vision. Sweet Goddess, the recent feeding had accomplished little more than to reduce the size and frequency of his stomach cramps.

He was fucking light-headed.

But as he reached the arched passage to the conservatory, he stood on the threshold and something in his heart started to ache.

Vojalie and Davido both stood to either side of Samantha, but very close, staring down into their new baby's face.

Samantha, holding Bernice, looked happy, much happier than at any time last night, but he'd noticed that infants often had that affect on females.

Right now, however, as a wave of nausea washed through him yet again, he wanted that to be his child, for Samantha to be wiping tears from her cheeks because of *their infant,* which of course made no sense at all. He hardly knew the woman, the daughter of Andrea who had betrayed him, as well as her kind, who could have prevented the tragedy at Sweet Gorge if she'd wanted to. Andrea had long-served Ethan's Guard with visions of imminent Invictus attacks and she would have had a vision of the attack at Sweet Gorge. But instead of contacting him, or any of his men, she'd abandoned Bergisson for good.

And his family had died.

These thoughts at least served to anchor him, to remind him why it would be best to let Samantha return as quickly as possible to Shreveport. His history with Andrea alone, was enough warning to keep the connection to Samantha at bay.

And all he needed to do was gain some control over Ry and she could leave his house and go where she wanted without danger of being kidnapped by a realm madman.

"Hey," he called out, straightening his shoulders. "I'm heading out. Just wanted to say good evening."

He thought he'd pulled it off, laced his words and movements with a casual air. But all three turned to stare at him, the tenderness of each expression giving way to wide-eyed shock.

Davido apparently spoke for them all. "Ethan, my good man, what the hell has happened to you? You're the shade of that Infidel, Dracula. By the Goddess's pink nipples, when was the last time you fed?"

"Just an hour ago, maybe less. Angela stopped by."

"Angela?" Samantha this time. She passed the infant to Vojalie. "Ethan, you had a *doneuse* here? Why didn't you come to me? I think I have enough blood right now to feed an army."

Ethan didn't know which was worse, that she would have willingly fed him but he'd missed the opportunity or the image of seeing her offer up her vein to an entire hoard of vampires.

He lost it. "Because it wasn't fucking appropriate, that's why?" His voice boomed through the conservatory. "You're my guest, not a donor. And, it doesn't matter. I'm fine."

As the scent of her drifted over to him, his mouth filled with saliva and it was all he could do not to groan long and loud. At the same time, probably because he'd been shouting, the baby started to cry.

Vojalie must have said something, because Davido put his feet in motion, hurried in his quick troll-like way, and caught Ethan's arm. He tugged him in the direction of the doorway. "Of course you're right. I spoke foolishly. Let's leave the women-folk with the baby. You're fine. You're fine. I can see that now. I take it you're off on patrol?"

"Yes." He wanted to turn back and apologize but Davido was doing for him what the social niceties would not allow him to do on his own; to make a much needed exit.

He let his friend usher him from the conservatory and out into the hall.

"Now that we're out of earshot of the ladies, let me be frank. You look bad, Ethan. I didn't want to alarm my wife or the lovely Samantha, but you're black-and-blue beneath your eyes and your skin is the color of goat's milk. Are you sure you're okay?"

"I'm fine or I will be once I get away from this latest nightmare. Shit, a blood rose. I was holding my own but her presence has made everything worse."

"Right, right. I'm sure you'll feel more fit when you leave the house. I can see how she must be the problem."

Davido took him all the way to the foyer and even opened the massive front door for him. "Goddess speed."

"And you." Then Ethan flew straight up into the air and didn't look back. The farther he got away from his house, and Samantha, the better he felt. The nausea passed and his stomach eased up. Sort of.

He met up with Finn near the Erishold Grotto, not far from the Fae Guildhall, but the look on his second-in-command's face told him the same story that Davido's had.

"I'm fine, damnit, now give me your report."

Chapter Four

"The Guildhall is very beautiful." Samantha lifted her gaze the entire height of the round, domed building. A narrower dome on top of the roof supported a golden minaret, on the pinnacle of which was the statue of a winged woman, an ancient mythical faery. "The lines of this building are unlike anything I've seen in my world, I mean the human world, except maybe Catalan architecture."

Vojalie had brought her to the fairgrounds and had already introduced her to a number of fae. What surprised Samantha the most was how everyone knew her mother, or of her, and was sorry to hear of her passing.

Sweeping a hand to encompass the front door, Vojalie said, "I think generally we prefer the arc, whether the circle, dome or archway. It's everywhere in our fae society. There's something very complete about it and I especially like the term 'full circle.'"

"You're thinking of me and my mother."

"Maybe. I'm also hoping that now that you're here you'll be able to solve the riddle about why she left. I've never completely understood."

"I'm hoping so as well." She turned to survey the grounds and was astonished all over again that they looked just as they had in her earlier vision. Dozens of colorful tents bearing flags on top rippled in the light, cool breeze, realm-folk moved about, haggling enthusiastically over prices, in the distance a fiddle and a flute played, and of course the smell of food was everywhere, constantly changing from booth to booth.

Because the vision looked just like this, she had every reason to believe that at some point the rest of the images would start unfolding as well, which kept Samantha's nerves on edge. When she'd shared her fears with Vojalie, that she was now living out the vision she'd foreseen, the woman had patted her shoulder reassuringly and said, "Trust me on this one thing: When the time comes, you will know exactly what needs to be done. It's the true gift of the vision, that the foreknowledge prepares the soul for future action. Trust in that."

The words comforted Samantha, because they gave her a logical solution to what was essentially a mystical situation. She just had to relax and let events unfold.

Vojalie had fed Bernice in a secluded corner of the park, a blanket draped over her shoulder, then Davido had taken her back to Ethan's house, in a taxi, where she would sleep for a couple of hours. Not all realm-folk could make use of levitated flight like Ethan and his powerful Guard.

A fae family approached Vojalie shyly, each bowing just a little, a very old, very formal greeting. Vojalie took the deference in stride then put her hand on the top of the children's heads, one after the other, which made them smile.

It occurred to Samantha that Vojalie might actually be doing something to them, so she asked.

Vojalie laughed. "It's a little trick, a soft jolt of vibration that sort of tickles. We call it a blessing and the children seem to love it."

"I'll bet they feel special."

Vojalie met and held her gaze. "I think so. I hope so. I don't think there's anything so important to a child as feeling special. And what of you? Did you feel that way growing up?"

Samantha wondered at the nature of the question. It seemed oddly personal, probing. "Yes, I did. Both my parents as well as my grandmother, gave me a lot of attention and love, but it was hard losing them all in the space of the past few years. At times, impossible."

"You have no other family?"

"No."

"So, in that sense, you could make a life for yourself here, in Bergisson, if you wanted to?"

She couldn't take the question in because the implications were so vast: Bergisson, realm-folk, her faeness, and always, Ethan and being a blood rose. "There are no impediments, just what's in my heart."

At that, Vojalie chuckled.

"What?"

"There is no impediment so great as what is in one's heart." She laughed again.

Samantha might have been irritated by the woman's amusement, but she had gained a sense of Vojalie that she carried no malice within her spirit, no jealousy, no mean-spiritedness. And what she'd said was true because if it wasn't in Samantha's heart to make a place for herself in Ethan's world, then nothing could move her here, not a dozen mastyrs, not a powerful fae, nothing.

The breeze picked up from the south and drove toward the distant northern hills, which were covered in large beech trees that shimmered against the dark night sky. She realized that her fae vision had continued to improve except for one small thing. "Am I seeing something red in the woods to the north?"

"What?" The sharpness of Vojalie's tone filled Samantha with sudden dread. "Oh, God, you're right. The Invictus are coming."

A moment later, the alarms sounded and realm-folk began gathering up children and heading straight for the Guildhall. "Come. We have an extensive underground system for just such an emergency."

Samantha realized this was just more of her vision unfolding as she continued to stare toward the trees.

Vojalie's phone rang. "No, my love. We're at the Guildhall. I'll be perfectly safe as you well know and yes, Samantha is with me." She tapped her phone, then returned it to the pocket of her tunic. "We should go."

But Samantha felt it now, or rather *him*. This was where her vision had picked up and she could feel the Mastyr of Bergisson's blood-hunger and the dire extent of his weakness.

Which meant that she had a very difficult decision to make.

"I have to stay."

"Do what you must." Then Vojalie was gone.

*** *** ***

Because of Samantha's vision, Ethan already had a large portion of his Guard at the fairgrounds, waiting near the eastern ridge, keeping a low profile among the trees, but he was in bad shape. Spots continued to move in and out of his vision and he fought an almost constant dizziness now. He knew he should turn the battle over to Finn, but the sight of the red wind had boosted his power and he'd flown down the eastern slopes at the front of his troops, his hand raised high, a war-cry in his throat.

He loathed the Invictus, those terrible, powerful wraith-based pairs that forged fighting units to challenge his men like nothing else could.

Through decades of practice, his men spread out in a long line across the grassy portion of the fairgrounds, setting up a defense between the beech-wood and all the colorful tents. Together his Guard would construct a shared wall of battle energy that would keep the Invictus from crossing. But they'd fight each Guardsmen with weapons of steel as well as streams of energy. If they could break through the powerful shield, they could attack the innocent at the Guildhall.

Something had to change in the way his Guard fought the Invictus. Ethan knew he needed a new mode of attack, maybe even a secondary attack strategy, something with grit, that personal touch lost with the development of the frequency support shields.

Though the shields served to keep the Invictus away from whatever population was nearby, something had been lost over the centuries in coming to terms with an enemy that simply never went away.

These thoughts shot through his head repeatedly as the Invictus pairs finally emerged from the woods, the horrible wraiths who had perverted themselves to take on a symbiotic mate, essentially enslaving another realm inhabitant. Wraiths often kidnapped realm-folk, of varying species, to forge a bonded pair and in that bonding, power surged. A weapon of war resulted, but to what army did this weapon belong?

He recalled Gerrod speaking of the Great Mastyr Vampire and an ancient fae force, but did these entities exist or had they been the imaginings reported by a wraith in the throes of death?

But the nature of the Invictus, as well as their consistent reappearance in each of the Nine Realms year after year, had long-convinced Ethan that some greater force lay behind the constant Invictus threat. The recent Merhaine attacks, with dramatically increased Invictus numbers, as well as the escalation in his own Bergisson Realm, showed organized strategy and tactics, the work of a master-mind.

"Steady!" His voice boomed down the ranks and an answering shout returned, echoing against the front line of the forest. They were fifty Guardsmen strong tonight, with the rest of his Guard out patrolling in every sector of his realm.

But this part of the battle he loved, the unity of his Guard, the brotherhood of warriors, fighting for their land and for their people, whom they served. He shouted with his men, great cries into the night, daring the enemy to test their mettle.

A new figure rose above the red wind, however, high into the air, cresting the tops of the trees. He felt Finn reach for him along his telepathic frequency and he opened up.

Are you seeing this? Finn's voice slid into his mind.

Ry. That bastard.

What the fuck does this mean? He can't have gone over to the Invictus?

Ethan had a hard time believing it as well. *And yet, I'm not surprised. I wonder how long this has been going on? Has he been betraying Bergisson all these years?*

I wouldn't put it past him.

Since the Invictus advanced, there was nothing more to be said and Ethan closed down the communication. He prepared himself for battle as the wraiths came into view.

Wraiths wore loose clothing, often made up of simple strips of fabric sewn together, to allow for movement in flight. They rarely walked on solid ground, but rather flew, levitated, or floated. They were almost always barefoot with spindly legs not meant for supporting their weight on land.

Ry didn't come down from the treetops, however, but remained levitating and smirking, arms over his chest. He wore leather pants and a black tee, his Guard uniform clearly a thing of the past. The Invictus pairs would do his bidding tonight, that much Ethan sensed, but why? What power did he have over them and how had he gained that level of command?

The Invictus advanced, a fierce line of wraith-pairs, a hundred strong tonight, which meant two hundred in number. Their mates came from all species but transformed so that even trolls held a fierce look and reddened eyes that indicated a bonding with a wraith. Steel weapons of all kinds appeared in ready hands.

Ethan gathered his remaining power, but even as he prepared to do battle, the spots at the edges of his vision increased and his dizziness swelled. When his stomach twisted into a knot, he knew he was in real trouble.

He opened his telepathy and pathed Finn once more. *Finn!*

I'm here, mastyr.

I've got a situation.

We've got a battle.

Close my gap, now. You're in charge.

Finn glanced at him. *Shit. Okay. No problem. Don't worry; I've got this.*

Ethan was falling backward at the same moment Finn closed up the battle shield. He heard Finn's voice as he started calling out orders.

But once more, his voice intruded. *Fuck, Ethan. We're in trouble. We've got at least a hundred pairs coming out of the forest and Ry is smiling. This was a planned attack and he knew the majority of your force would be out on their patrols.*

Ethan's consciousness wavered but he felt the decision come together in his mind like a powerful magnet pulling the pieces to each other. He hadn't wanted to do this, but he knew now that without Samantha's help, his force would perish tonight, the Guildhall would be overrun, and hundreds of innocents would die.

He opened his telepathic frequency again, only this time he focused on Samantha. *Can you hear me?*

A pause, then, *I hear you, Ethan.*

I need you. I need you to serve me. I didn't want to infringe on your freedom, but can you come to me? It'll be dangerous, but can you come?

Already heading in your direction.

Thank the Goddess. The spots grew larger and he closed his eyes. He couldn't even hear the battle anymore.

*** *** ***

The moment Samantha had seen Ethan fall, she'd started running. She hadn't joined Vojalie and the others in the shelter, not when she was watching the vision from the prave play out in front of her eyes, not when she knew what would happen, not when she saw Ethan fall.

Vojalie, to her credit, had left Samantha alone to follow her own path.

The field felt like an unlimited distance, however, that kept increasing as the battle raged. Blue and red streams of light flashed everywhere and she kept hearing the wraiths shriek, a sound that sent chills through her.

One of the end Guardsmen suddenly broke away from the battle and headed in her direction. She understood and shifted course to meet him, her arms pumping hard. Her heart had never felt so weighed down, so ready to burst.

When the Guardsman drew close, she lifted her arms while still running. He caught her easily, flew her the distance to Ethan in a matter of seconds, then dropped her to the grass beside him. He took off almost in the same moment, heading back to his position in the ranks.

But the Bergisson mastyr was as pale as death.

"Ethan," she called out, kneeling next to him.

His head moved slightly, but he wouldn't open his eyes, wouldn't wake up. She couldn't feed him by herself; he'd need to participate. She struck him across the face with her hand once then twice.

When his eyes opened and he saw her, she lay down beside him and placed her wrist over his mouth. He met and held her gaze as his fangs struck.

A sting then heavy pulls on her arm. He groaned at the same time.

The battle raged on so that she didn't think about what Ethan was doing, but watched in horror as wraiths screamed high-pitched battle sounds and threw weapons in precise patterns at each of the Guardsmen. But when caught by an answering stream of Guard battle-energy, chests smoked and imploded, blood flew in horrifying arcs and their mates cried out as if in terrible pain, maybe dying with the wraiths.

She'd never seen so much violence or gore in her life.

Look at me.

Ethan's voice cut through the agony around her. She turned her head and met his gaze.

He continued, *Look only at me. Don't think about what's happening out there. Close your eyes if you need to.*

She blocked the sounds of the battle, then closed her eyes. She pictured the cottage by the lake, the one she'd envisioned since childhood although in those visions she always saw her mother waving to her, beckoning her to come to her. How pretty her mother looked in this fantasy, with a blue dress that went clear to the ground, an old-fashioned gown from a hundred years ago, almost peasant-like.

No, more like Vojalie's tunic. More *fae*-like.

How much she missed her.

The cottage had smooth river-rock all around the base, then dark beams and plaster above, and wood-shingle roof. A garden gate with a climbing rose over a trellis heralded the vegetable garden at the side of the house. Weeping willows graced a vast lawn on both sides of the property. A dock went out several yards into the lake.

She'd love to live there someday.

Arms suddenly scooped her up, but not Ethan's. The same Guardsman who'd brought her to him, now carried her away.

She twisted in his arms, to glance back at Ethan. He stood tall and clear-eyed: strong. He waved to her with a short lift of his hand then turned back once more to engage the enemy. He'd been completely restored.

She'd done that. She'd been of service. She'd helped.

She'd also opened a door, crossing from spectator to participant. She doubted she'd be able to shut that door.

As the Guardsman dropped her by the Guildhall, she turned once more to watch him levitate and shoot into the air. She hadn't wanted this, but here she was, in Bergisson, having just fed a mastyr vampire and she'd never felt better in her life.

She had no idea what the future held, but Shreveport somehow seemed like a faraway place and definitely a world apart.

*** *** ***

Ethan's renewed strength sent shockwaves down both sides of the Guard's joint shield, which resulted in a series of whoops.

Like music to Ethan's ears.

He'd never felt more alive, more powerful.

Beams of energy flew from the tips of his fingers in lightning flashes, stronger and more lethal than ever before. Many of the pairs began to drop where they stood, and after a few minutes more, the Invictus line began to retreat in stages.

The Guardsman to his right gave a heavy groan. He'd taken a blade to his upper chest, high enough to have escaped lungs or heart. Ethan retaliated, and sent a strong stream of power straight for the offending wraith's right eye. The wraith screamed as he fell from levitated flight, his body hitting the earth with a thud and twitching. His mate, a female troll dropped to the earth as well, her eyes rolling in her head.

Ethan saw her shudder and thought she might have murmured, 'I'm free' as she died, but couldn't be certain.

He continued battling, his strength never wavering, a phenomenal circumstance alone given the acute suffering of the past several weeks. Had his body somehow known that his blood rose existed out there, had been calling to her all this time?

He caught one last glimpse of the traitor, Ry, his eyes narrowed and hard as he met and held Ethan's gaze. The promise of vengeance radiated from Ry's expression, the set of his jaw, and the reddening of his dark eyes. He moved fast, and soon disappeared beyond the canopy of the beech-wood.

A horn sounded in the distance, a sound Ethan had never heard before. The Invictus had, however. Those remaining wraith-pairs, at least fifty in number, and as if trained to respond instantly, turned and shot back into the depths of the woodland, leaving their dead and wounded behind.

His suspicions that something, or someone, had brought an increased degree of order to the wraith-pair ranks, had just been proved here on the field. Clearly, Ry was involved, but knowing Ry as he did, Ethan doubted that the traitor had achieved this level of organization alone.

So, who were the mastyrs of the Nine Realms really battling in what appeared to be an escalating war against a growing Invictus offensive?

He turned to Finn, stationed beside him, and despite the horror of those lives lost, his second-in-command smiled then pathed, *You look a helluva lot better, my friend.*

Ethan nodded. To merely say he felt better seemed like so much less than what needed to be said, what should be honored. His blood rose, a woman he'd met just over twenty-four hours ago, had crossed to the frontlines of a battlefield and fed him, not only saving his life but providing Ethan with enough added power to alter and undoubtedly shorten the duration of the fairground battle.

It's over, was all he could think to say. His gaze drifted to the wraith-corpses, to their mates of varying species who'd been harnessed to a wraith against his or her will. Yes, there were women on the field, even less able than the men to have withstood a wraith subjugation.

He went to the troll he'd observed fall and murmur something, but when he reached her, she'd already passed on. Sometimes the separation occurring from the death of the wraith set in motion the demise of the mate. The troll was very thin and covered in bruises. Around her neck was a locket.

He opened it and saw the pictures of a boy and girl, the smiling photos taken at elementary school. But the pictures looked old, which meant the woman had been bound to a wraith for a long time.

He didn't care about the why of this tragedy, only that it still existed in his realm and he wanted this kind of enslavement to end.

Many of those fae with healing gifts were already running or engaging in levitated flight to cross the expanse of lawn, that stretch near the Guildhall where soccer was played every weekend through the inter-species league.

His might be a kingdom with a warring enemy, but his people pitched in as dozens, no hundreds of realm-folk came to care for his injured Guardsmen and the wounded among the wraith-pairs.

Finn and another of his Guard, Kyle, went from fallen Invictus pair to the next in order to determine if either wraiths or the mates survived. The wounded wraiths would be taken to a prison hospital as would any mates found to be hostile or beyond reach.

Those mates who had been obviously subjugated against their will and who survived the death of the wraith, were given priority and rushed first to the fae with the greatest healing gifts as well as the realm-surgeons as needed.

Several of his Guard patrolled the edge of the beech-wood to make sure the enemy had truly quit the field. Ethan only had to learn once the hard way that sometimes the retreat was a feint.

The corpses were gathered and taken to various morgues.

When the battlefield saw the last bit of debris hauled away, including the grass washed free of blood and any other battle-related detritus, like pieces of burnt clothing and scattered weapons, only then did Ethan finally levitate into the air and begin a slow progression in the direction of the Guildhall and Samantha.

A single thought of Samantha, however, put his heart in high gear. Having taken her blood had changed everything and now that the battle was over, his body seemed lit up and ready just for her.

He took deep breaths because what he needed from her now had nothing to do with a deep draw at her neck. But Goddess help him, how could he ask even more of her?

*** *** ***

Samantha wanted to go home, back to Shreveport.

This was all too much.

She stood in the shadows of the Guildhall, having watched the last of the fae healers, the physicians, and the support volunteers depart the field so that now only Ethan and his Guard remained.

And Ethan moved slowly in her direction.

She felt him coming for her like a slow-moving ocean wave, something she couldn't stop even if she'd wanted to.

She'd fed Ethan and he'd battled his enemy, maybe even saving the day, or the *night*, so to speak. But this wasn't her fight or her war. She was human, too, not just fae, not just a blood rose. Why should this be her fate?

Earlier, families with children and the aged had gone home as soon as a member of the Guard told them it was safe, scattering quickly to either cars in the parking lot or taking off in levitated-flight. Many of the realm-folk could fly, but a good number relied on more traditional forms of transportation. Those who had arrived at the fairgrounds on bicycles arranged to travel in cars with supportive friends and family members.

The grass looked pristine in the glow of her new realm-vision.

What had taken place, once the battle ended, had been accomplished by the local realm-folk by long habit, a story all in itself.

The Invictus had tormented the Nine Realms for centuries and no matter how many wraith-pairs were killed, more arrived to replace each lost unit. Vojalie's insights into Bergisson's daily life flowed through her mind, of how hard the community of a million souls strived to live each day as normal as possible despite the constant threat of an unpredictable enemy.

As Ethan drew near, she couldn't believe how much better he looked. The blue beneath his eyes had vanished and his complexion now had a golden, tanned appearance instead of the chalk she'd witnessed even at the prave.

"You're better." She wished he wasn't, wished her blood hadn't been good for him, but the evidence of what she was stood right in front of her.

Because of the battle, his long hair had come loose from the woven clasp that held it in place. Curls and strands flowed away from his face and her heart thrummed all over again, getting ready for him if he needed her. He shouldn't be so beautiful. He should be thin, pale and evil-looking instead of towering over her like a god from mythology.

"You're alone?" Ethan scowled.

"I sent Vojalie back to your house as soon as the Invictus left. The baby needed her."

"But there's no one else here." He glanced beyond her to the Guildhall.

"I felt secure enough because your Guardsmen are still patrolling."

"I don't like that you're alone. You should have gone with Vojalie."

Did he have to be so worried for her safety?

Tears filled her eyes and she was ready to launch into all her reasons for why she wanted him, right this minute, to take her back to Shreveport. But he stepped close and took her arm gently in his hand and squeezed. "Thank you."

Her breath caught and held. "You don't have to say that, not to me, not for this."

"Yes, I do. I didn't have time to tell you before. Thank you for saving my life. In fact, because of what you did, you saved hundreds of lives tonight, not just mine."

She was taken aback. "Is that what I did?"

He nodded. "I don't know why, but I wasn't far from death. I didn't realize it until you came to me, until I started to feed. I'm stubborn in that way. I don't always understand the most basic things."

At the time that she'd crossed the field to him, she'd felt so confident about doing what was needed to be done, just as Vojalie had said she would feel. But why did it all have to be about life-and-death?

"I want you to find someone else." There she'd said it.

"I know. I can feel it in you, that you're unhappy about what happened, that you feel trapped, and I'll do whatever you say because I believe in your right to whatever path you want to follow.

"But I also believe in my heart that you've come into my realm for a reason. I think Bergisson needs you but I don't know in what way. I realize we have this issue between us, or maybe it would be better to say that I have this critical need for you right now, but that doesn't have to define the future.

"However, just for the time being, I'm asking you to stay, until I can get this all figured out, especially Ry. He's the threat that most concerns me and that his drive toward you, now that he's seen what you can do, is probably stronger than ever. Do you understand? Ry was here at the battle. He's joined the Invictus and he watched you feed me."

She nodded, but something inside her collapsed, a feeling that her liberty was being eroded. Was this how her mother had felt all those years, maybe enslaved in service to Bergisson because of her inherent fae power, something she'd been born with but never chosen?

His voice was softer now as he rubbed her arm. "Please stay." Because of her fae abilities, she could sense his desperation. "I haven't felt well like this in fifty years."

"Okay, that doesn't help at all. Are you trying to guilt me into this?"

"No, dear Goddess, no. I'm just trying to explain all the reasons why, if I can find some way to duplicate what you've given me, I need to do that."

"So now you want to duplicate my blood?"

"Look, it's clear to me that you don't want to be here. I get it. You are your mother's daughter. I'm just asking for you to stick around for a few days."

"What if it turns into weeks or months?"

He seemed startled, like he hadn't considered that as a possibility, then she understood the flip side of this coin. "Oh, my God, you don't really want me to stay, either?"

He fell silent and his hand dropped away. His gaze shifted off to the side and his scowl deepened. "I have a duty to perform here in my realm that makes it impossible for me to become involved with any woman. When I first saw you, and felt you connect with my personal frequency, I knew you were going to be a problem."

"I don't fit into your plans." She should have been miffed, instead she felt relieved. "That's good."

His gaze shifted back to her. "How is that good?"

"Because now I know we have the same goal, to get me back to Shreveport when all this is over."

He nodded and then he smiled. "Yes, we have the same goal."

Samantha took a deep breath, the first one since she'd fed Ethan and watched her blood fire him up like she'd put caffeine straight into his veins. But it was his smile that shifted the direction of the exchange, like a train being rerouted by a simple switch of the tracks.

Ethan had a great smile. He probably knew it as well, but right now all she saw was the reflection of her own sense of relief, that each had stated a simple desire not to engage, and so she could breathe and Ethan could smile.

His gaze caught and held, however, and she felt his personal frequency streaming toward her begging for a connection. The fae part of her received that frequency and her body lit up. His hillside grassy scent thickened in the air and tightened her abdomen. Her lips parted like she needed to say something, but nothing came out.

"Samantha," he whispered, his voice hoarse and deep.

"If we did this, it changes nothing, right?"

He nodded, brisk hopeful jerks of his head. "Right. Nothing. Just mutual enjoyment, fulfillment of need."

Her turn to nod. She cleared her throat. "But you need to get back to the patrols."

"Yes. I'll be home at dawn."

Sunrise seemed about a million hours away when what she wanted was right in front of her.

"Ethan?" The Guardsman, Finn, called out, heading in their direction.

Ethan's nostrils flared and a look of irritation then amusement crossed his face. To her, he said, "I'll get you home then meet you later?"

"I'll be waiting."

Ethan turned to Finn just as he touched down a few feet away. "I have to get Samantha home."

"Let one of the Guard do it."

Though she was looking at Ethan's back, she felt his sudden tension like multiple waves beating at her chest all at once. "No, Finn. I have to do this."

Samantha stepped around Ethan and inclined her head to Finn. He returned the gesture but he was scowling. He seemed to disapprove, but she wasn't sure why. He said nothing more, but turned and flew back in the direction of the woodland, his leather coat flapping behind him. "What was that about?"

"What was what?"

"Why didn't you let one of the other Guardsmen see me home? I mean, maybe Finn felt you would be more valuable here."

Ethan looked down at her and opened one arm, extending his right booted foot just a little. She knew the drill. As she slid her arm around his neck, she balanced both feet on the top of his foot. Left to herself, she was sure she'd fall, but his arm clamped around her waist like a vise.

He leaned close and straight into her ear, whispered, "Want to know why? Because I'd kill any man for getting this close to you right now. Understand?"

His warm breath and the resonance of his voice filled her ear and sent a series of shivers cascading over her neck and shoulders and down her back. Desire flooded her, so that she could do nothing else but turn toward his mouth and catch his lips with her own.

A growl filled his throat as he drove his tongue inside her mouth. She'd been longing for this kiss, and much more, from the moment she'd first seen him storm into Club Prave. She hadn't been with a man in so long.

I want you now. Even his voice in her head filled her with strange, realm vibrations, one after the other, heightening the passion that flowed through her like music.

You'd better just take me home.

But his mouth moved over hers like he had no intention of stopping, his tongue plunging in and out, making all sorts of promises.

She couldn't help what happened next as she turned into him, sliding her other arm around his neck.

He pulled her hard against him and dipped low to caress her bottom, pressing her hips into what was hard and ready for her. If she'd been in doubt about his size, she felt everything right now, that he would fill her up and then some, which weakened her knees even more, then flooded her mind with new doubts about how easy it would be for her to leave Bergisson.

He drew back, his eyes glittering in the dark. "Let's go."

She didn't remember the ride, only that her nose kept sniffing the leather of his uniform and the tangy male scent of his neck. By the time he touched down in front of his house, she'd started sucking on his neck and he'd pulled her against him once more.

*** *** ***

Ethan didn't know how he was going to separate from Samantha, but Finn's voice asked telepathic admittance.

He drew back from her about two full inches, unwilling to release her, when Finn pathed, *I followed you just to make sure Ry didn't have a secondary plan in place. Take her inside. We've got this.*

Maybe it was the amusement in Finn's voice, or the trace of masculine sympathy for Ethan's current plight, but Ethan finally relented. *I'll check in later.*

No. Check in tomorrow evening. I'm telling you, I've got this. Your Guard is well-trained, the best in the Nine Realms. We can do without you for one night, you love-starved bastard.

Did anyone ever tell you that you can be a real dick?

Just my wife, at least once a night.

Ethan was still undecided until Samantha found his neck again and once more started to suck just over his vein. Did she know how that made him feel? Maybe. Probably.

Oh, hell. Call me if you need me, no matter how small the problem Got it?

Yes, Mastyr.

Ethan chuckled and ended the pathing call.

He lifted Samantha's chin and she left his neck with a small smacking sound. He kissed her, then scooped her up in his arms. "I'm taking you to bed. Now."

Her eyes opened wide. "You sure? Now? What about your men?"

"I just cleared it with Finn."

She drew in a soft breath. "Well, then."

Chapter Five

Ethan carried Samantha up both short flights of stairs, through the sitting room and down the long hall in the direction of his suite. Fortunately, Vojalie and her family were settled in one of the south suites off the family room, a good distance from his west-facing bedroom.

He trembled, as much from what was about to happen as by the reality that he'd never wanted a woman in his rooms before the way he wanted her.

She'd drawn close again and had her lips on his neck, tonguing his skin, then sucking. He wanted those same lips down low and doing the same thing.

He shuddered.

She'd feed him again. He knew it without having to really think about it. He could feel her heart pounding heavily, her veins full of what he needed. He wanted to be moving into her slowly this time as he pinned her shoulders to the bed and drank from her, his hips curling with each thrust to keep the whole act perfect and coordinated. He wanted to come with his mouth drinking down her essence.

His personal frequency vibrated heavily now and the part of her that was fae responded so that in the center of his being, another layer of sensation kept him hard, worked up, and on fire.

He shoved open the door to his suite, then kicked it closed behind him.

The room opened up to either side, but he headed for the open shower, in a large alcove between, flanked on one side by an indoor garden. The cool, humid air brought Samantha away from him and turning in his arms.

"This is your bathroom? Your shower?" She turned to stare at him. "You have a garden in here?"

"I do." He started stripping out of his Guard uniform, dropping the coat on the hardwood floor, then easing out of his shirt.

Her eyes flared. Her frequency stroked him first then her hands followed as she splayed her fingers over his abs then slowly moved up, covering his pecs to rise and fondle his shoulders. Leaning into him, she sucked his left nipple, then his right, then back and forth until his eyes rolled in his head and he groaned.

If just her touch, and her lips flicking each tip, sent this much desire through him, what would the rest be like? She leaned into him, sucking harder. *You taste like war,* she pathed through his mind.

He groaned all over again.

He reached over her back and found the bottom of her shirt and started to pull upward. She drew back and lifted her arms overhead. Not waiting, she got rid of her shoes and jeans, the rest of her female gear.

For a split-second, he debated whether to attack her or take the time to lose his boots and leathers. Like the smart man he was, he got rid of the last hindrance to both the shower and her body.

He cranked up the jets and as he got the temperature just right, he turned to find her eyes wide once more as her gaze drifted up and down his ass.

"Ethan, you're magnificent." She moved toward him and he stayed right where he was. Again, another sign of his basic intelligence.

She dropped down behind him and started kissed his left ass-cheek, then shifted to his right, then went lower until she was kissing the backs of his thighs. He spread his legs, water pouring down his chest. Her fingers drifted over his balls and in front to stroke upward as she fondled what was getting way too hard.

The whole time, a vibration worked over his skin from her touch, something very realm, but which he'd never experienced before. This was something uniquely Samantha.

His blood rose. A half-fae with more power than most of the full-fae he knew.

A woman who had with one feeding, ended decades of suffering. His stomach no longer cramped and he felt whole and strong.

But he needed to calm down.

"Let's change things up."

As he turned, she rose up off her knees, her light blue eyes darkening with passion. Her fingertips grazed the front of his thighs. He put his hands on her shoulders. "Will you scrub some of the battle sweat off me?"

She nodded, found a bar of French-milled soap in the tile inset, and set to work. She foamed up her hands, handed him the bar and began to rub in circles over his neck and chest, his shoulders and arms. Down she went. He closed his eyes as her hands covered every inch of his skin, even down to his toes.

"Turn," she commanded. "And give me the soap again."

He obeyed, and had the pleasure of feeling the rest of him lathered up, from ankles to ass to the breadth of his back, and beneath the long length of his heavy, wet hair, until she was done.

He turned in the spray of the shower to face her.

With a crooked smile and the soap in her hand held palm up, she said, "Do me."

He smiled, he couldn't help it. "With pleasure."

*** *** ***

Samantha had slipped into a place she'd never been before, a part of herself undiscovered until now. For one thing, her body sang, that was the only way she could explain it. She knew the realm-world was a world of frequency and vibration, but now she experienced a part of that reality. His frequency flowed over her in waves, like the softest touch caressing her skin with continual erotic pulses, while deep within, she felt the response of her own fae frequency, reaching for his vibration, entwining at times, engaging.

But there was another part that had more to do with her human experiences in that right now she felt irrationally free of inhibitions with a man who was just shy of being a stranger to her.

She'd had sex with more than one of her boyfriends, but it had never been like this. Of course, Ethan was beyond the norm, so far beyond what she'd known that she was sure only the realm-world could have produced such a man.

He smiled, that extraordinary smile of his, made even broader because his thick curly hair lay wet and flat against his head, setting his features in beautiful relief; his cheekbones powerful, his jaw firm, and the indentation of his chin inviting her tongue.

She almost leaned up to take a swipe, but suddenly Ethan's hands, full of lather, were planted on her breasts. Her back arched, which thrust her chest forward. Ethan leaned in, his big hands covering and fondling her, his fingers rising to peaks and tugging on her now-firm nipples. The lubricant of the soap made the sensation soft, fiery, and sensual all at the same time.

She closed her eyes, her hands balanced on his hips so she wouldn't fall. He massaged harder and harder and she pressed into him, until her hips undulated and her internal well pulled on what she needed to be there, the sooner the better.

He slid one hand low and he soaped her between her legs, rubbing slowly and carefully. He took pains to rinse her off as well. "I want you in my bed."

The words came out like a command, which tightened her abdomen and her breathing hitched. He dried them both off carefully with a thick tower, then cupped her face and kissed her once, afterward searching her eyes. "Am I pleasing you?"

She gave a soft cry, stunned that he would be concerned, then threw her arms around his neck, plastering herself against him.

He responded, surrounding her with all that muscle and strength, his arms overlapping her back.

For a heady second she swore she could stay like this forever, in the circle of his caring embrace and the strength of his warrior's body.

He chuckled, which became a jarring motion against his chest. "I take that as a yes."

Yes, she pathed, sliding her thoughts over his.

He met her gaze again. *I love that you can penetrate my mind like this.*

She nodded, still clinging to him. *All this faeness that I'm discovering. It's amazing.*

He lifted her off her feet and in that odd dangling position he kissed her repeatedly as he carried her into his sleeping area that also opened up to the large enclosed garden. While still holding her, he pulled back the comforter and laid her down easily on his bed, as though she was a feather, another sign that he wasn't human, that he had more physical strength than she could imagine.

She thought he would stretch out on top of her, instead, he caught her calves, one in each hand, and pulled her to the side of the bed. Her body went lax knowing full well what he meant to do.

I love your landing strip, penetrated her mind, as he dropped to his knees, *black like your hair.* Then he went to work. She closed her eyes and gave herself to the sensation of Ethan's soft, moist tongue as he laved her folds, teased her lips, and flicked the center of her, where the pleasure was most intense.

Soft coos and moans left her throat and as he increased the pressure and speed, her hips rose and fell, over and over, her well clenching with need. He worked her slow, then fast, then slow, prolonging the moment and the experience, but ushering her steadily toward the pinnacle.

His left hand held her in place as he supported her bottom, but his right hand began a lengthy exploration of her thighs and mound, her abdomen and upward to fondle her breasts. All the while his tongue licked and pleasured her.

At the same time, his vibrations rolled, another layer of sensation so that her mind became lost, falling deeper and deeper as ecstasy hurtled toward her, sharpening the pleasure where his tongue touched and flicked until the orgasm rolled through her.

She cried out, but he didn't stop. He kept flicking until the waves of pleasure rose repeatedly, taking her to the heights again and again. After the last of her cries left her throat, she settled down and her hips relaxed back into the bed.

He looked up at her, his smile crooked. "Good?"

Her back arched as she reached down for him. "Unbelievable. The waves you sent through me, reached deep inside here…" She pressed her lower abdomen. "And here…" She drifted her fingers up to her heart. She laughed softly and held her hands up to him. "More?"

He rose up from his kneeling position and with his hands around her waist he told her to hold onto his arms. Doing as she was instructed, he lifted her easily farther up on the bed.

When he moved upward to join her, she spread her legs so that his knees could go between. He made an approving grunting sound, which made her laugh. And this was something she hadn't expected with Ethan, the good will and laughter, that he found things amusing and didn't mind when she did as well.

Planting his elbows on either side of her, he said, "You smell like raspberries and wine, did I tell you that?"

She shook her head. "Yes and your scent is wonderful as well, like something wild that grows on a mountainside; earthy, grassy, tangy. Your sweat was like that, when you flew me here."

"You didn't mind? You said I tasted like war."

"Uh-huh, like a man who'd just fought and saved hundreds of lives."

His chest rose and fell, his gaze sliding around to land once more on hers. "And you were part of that."

"I was. But it seemed like such a small service, to offer up a vein."

He shifted to stare down at her neck. "I need more and I can feel you're ripe again."

"I am."

He ran his thumb down her throat then licked the skin in a long line straight up to her ear.

"I can smell your blood, an erotic elixir now, because you've known pleasure." He trembled. "I want to be inside you when I drink."

"Yes." Her voice was breathy, hardly there. Her hips rolled, seeking.

He lowered himself onto her, using a hand to position himself at her entrance. "You're wet."

"I want you, Ethan. All of you, every inch. Now." Where had all this boldness come from?

"You've got me."

*** *** ***

Ethan pushed, slowly at first. She was tight, but then he was big and not every woman could handle what he had to give. But her groans, and the way she caught his ass and pulled him into her, encouraged him to push harder.

A hoarse moan helped him to know he was good. With his gaze fixed on the pulse in her throat, his chest tightened and his mouth watered. Her wrist had been one thing, but this would be better, much better.

Slowly his hips moved, driving farther each time, deeper.

Using his fingers, he pushed the long strands of her black hair away from her pale neck. She had a fae's complexion, very light and creamy.

Samantha was beautiful.

He leaned down and kissed the line of her jaw then her lips as he progressed inside her.

She pulled on him, her hands gripping his shoulders. "You feel so good, Ethan. So good." Her neck arched and her head slid up into the pillow, then back, a pure reflection of how his movements kept her body undulating slowly.

Her fingers squeezed his biceps, which caused his muscles to flex then relax. His vibration pulsed heavily now, swarming through her and touching her faeness. The sensation tightened his stomach and his ass.

Ethan. Her voice sounded soft inside his mind.

He met her gaze and thumbed her cheek. *I'm here.*

She smiled. *This is beautiful. Whatever our lives become, this moment is beautiful. I love being connected to you like this and your vibration has me worked up. It's amazing.*

Her words in his mind swelled his heart and ignited his personal frequency further so that new waves poured from him.

Oh, my God. What are you doing to me?

I'm not sure. He kissed her again. Waves pulsed from his chest and reached inside. *Focus on your faeness, your fae frequency and let it flow toward me. I think we can do something here, the two of us.*

She nodded.

Did the bed just tremble?

She closed her eyes, her lips parting wide as though caught in supreme ecstasy. Then he felt it as his frequency returned to him, but this time joined to hers. Pleasure, like he'd never known, spread fire through his chest, his stomach, and into his groin.

His hips moved faster, gliding easily within her because she rained on him now.

I need to drink.

Yes, drink. Ethan, please. I want you to. I need you to. She arched her neck, exposing a vein that rose from him.

He placed an arm over her left shoulder to keep her pinned. At the same time, by long practice, his hips moved so that he plunged in and out.

Turning his head and angling, he made a sharp jab with his fangs and surrounded the wounds with his lips. The first draw of raspberry-and-wine nectar exploded on his tongue. He groaned against her throat. He sucked hard and plunged faster and faster.

The sensation of their shared frequencies kept his chest on fire and his groin wicked with sensation and drive.

Her moans filled his ears.

So, close. I'm close again. The vibrations, my God. Ethan, my God.

Let it go.

She cried out and her well tugged on him as he worked her with his cock, as he drank from her, as he sent his frequency vibrating through her body, as he felt hers return and stroke him.

Her cries repeated, as though the orgasm rolled on and on and maybe it did. He was so hard, so ready.

I need to come.

Ethan, come. Yes, come, while you're drinking me down.

Those words did him in. His back tensed, his buttocks flexed and his balls released. He pumped faster while still sucking at her neck. Pleasure rode his cock and because she cried out, her hips meeting his with answering grinds, he knew another orgasm carried her along, which intensified what he felt, the nerve endings singing and shouting ecstasy.

But he wasn't done and their shared frequency rose to intensify every sensation.

He kept rocking into her.

Her voice was in his head once more. *I'll come again if you keep doing that.*

And you'll bring me again.

Yes, please. Do that, only can you look at me this time?

He left her neck, his body now full of her life-blood, his veins whirring in response, their joined frequencies firing him up.

He planted his hands on either side of her, lifting up so he could see her and focused on driving into her. She touched his face, his cheeks, his lips. She breathed in quick gasps, her body undulating beneath his.

"Our frequencies, as though my body is trembling head-to-foot--"

"I know."

He went faster, his vampire ability surpassing what a human could do. Her mouth remained open as though she struggled for air. She became very still beneath him, just feeling him. Her light blue eyes shone in the dark room.

She gasped.

Are you coming.

Yes.

How he loved telepathy in moments like this and she was powerful enough to make it easy.

A second orgasm shot through him. He arched away from her roaring this time because the sensation, doubling over the earlier one, felt like pleasurable fire through his cock as he released into her. She gripped his arms, crying out again and again. Ecstasy streamed a conversation between them, of pleasuring rising to the heights repeatedly.

Sex had never been like this before, not in his long-lived life, not ever. She cried out over and over, whimpering, and grasping him from within.

Finally, the sensations slid down the other side of the hill and her hips settled into the bed. He rested on top of her, still holding himself up. He was breathing hard, so was she.

She thumbed his lips. "You have my blood."

He nodded as a kind of lethargy overtook him. He wanted to roll over and lie on his back, maybe just fall asleep. But at the same time, he didn't want to leave her body.

Instinctively, he knew that the moment he did, everything would change as it always did after sex, sometimes better, sometimes worse. But mostly, he didn't want to sever the connection he felt to her.

Then he realized that his frequency was still communing with hers.

"What is it?" she asked.

"We're still connected? Can you feel the vibration?"

"Yes, but I thought it was a kind of afterglow."

He smiled. "Maybe it is, but we're still joined, my mating frequency to your fae vibration."

She grabbed both ass-cheeks and pushed against him. "And we're joined here, as well."

He chuckled. She made him laugh. He tried to remember the last time a woman had done that for him.

She tilted her head. "I want to explore the vibration connection. Is that okay?"

He dipped his chin. "Anything you want."

She closed her eyes and he felt her focus on their shared frequency. *It feels really solid, that 'joined' is the right word.*

I agree.

Can it come apart? I mean how? You've done this before, right?

No, I haven't.

At that, her eyes popped wide. "Somehow, I had the impression this was the way things were done."

"Every couple is different and some of that difference comes with specie; my vampire to your fae and to your humanness."

"I see, sort of. Would you mind if I tried to disconnect? I don't want to, but I'm so intrigued."

He didn't want it either, but he liked the sparkle in her eye a lot. "Go for it."

She closed her eyes once more and took deep breaths. Slowly she released his frequency and it felt like fingers unclasping and pulling away, like they'd been holding hands but had to let go.

His first impulse was to stop her. He didn't want her to go and yet she couldn't remain attached like this. He tried something similar, just a focused release and the same thing happened, a kind of unfurling of his frequency and a slow, peaceful, almost satisfied, separation.

It seemed appropriate to withdraw from her body at the same time.

Of course, this left a different kind of issue to resolve and he left the bed to get a washcloth and bring it back to her.

"Do it for me," she said, smiling, her eyes sleepy.

He opened up the cloth and pressed it between her legs. He leaned down and because he was grateful for so much of what had transpired between them, he kissed her mound.

She petted his head, still damp from the shower.

He crawled beneath the covers, then slid to lie down beside her, covering her at the same time.

"Thank you, that feels good. I got chilled so fast once you weren't near me."

"I could sense you were cold."

"You could?"

"Yeah." He settled his elbow on the pillow and planted his head in his hand so he could look down at her. He liked the view. "I can sense your satisfaction right now. Must be a frequency thing, your faeness, maybe."

"You satisfied me." She held up her left hand, splaying her fingers slightly. He met her hand, with his own, joining his fingers with hers.

Glancing at their hands, she wrinkled up her nose. "This is what our frequencies felt like to me."

"Me, too, exactly, entwined. This is a strong way to hold another person's hand."

She chuckled softly, then met his gaze once more. "For a moment there, I wasn't sure we'd be able to separate."

The statement caught him up short and made him think of his world, his realm, his duties as Mastyr of Bergisson. He had to admit that what he'd just experienced with Samantha existed outside of anything he'd ever known before. He feared exactly what she'd just stated, an implication that if they continued making love like this, if he kept drinking from her, feeling so possessive about her, would he only make the inevitable parting an impossibility later down the road?

"I can almost hear your thoughts." She pulled her hand away and his fingers relaxed, letting her slide from his grasp. "We can't really go on like this. It's too much."

"I know."

She heaved a sigh as she turned away from him to lie on her side.

But he put his hand on her shoulder, sliding down her arm, then moved in to spoon her. "I know. You're absolutely right."

She covered his forearm with her hand and sighed once more.

*** *** ***

Samantha had mixed feelings. On the one hand, she'd turned away from him knowing that she needed to keep things light between them. But maybe she'd done it too quickly, because it felt like a door shutting too fast, not quite a slam, but near enough.

Though Ethan now spooned her, she could tell he'd shut down as well. But this kind of intense coupling reminded her of the descriptions her girlfriends would give of honeymoon experiences, but she barely knew Ethan and he was a different species, neither human nor fae.

And she was just getting used to being something that she'd never known about in her twenty-eight years of living on the planet.

He cleared his throat. "Hey, I loved what we just did."

"I know. Me, too." She yawned and patted his arm. "It's okay. We have a lot to figure out in the next few days, but right now, I think I need some sleep."

"Good idea."

Though Samantha felt unsettled by the awkwardness of the moment, the fatigue of the night fell on her and she drifted into a deep sleep.

*** *** ***

The next afternoon, Ethan awoke to an empty bed and his first thought was something close to panic. His concern for Samantha's safety rode his nerves constantly, from the time Ry had shown up outside her Shreveport house.

He sat up and looked around, listening intently into the depths of the house, but everything sounded normal. He released a deep sigh and slid his legs over the side of the bed.

He knew his household well, that his staff would have already made Samantha, as well as Vojalie and Davido, feel welcome. Because he had a state-of-the-art security system, and all vampires were still indoors at this hour, he let his fears slide away. Even wraiths had a certain sensitivity to sunlight. At least for now, Samantha was safe.

His clothes still lay where he'd dropped them and he smiled. He crossed to his leathers and found his phone. Calling Finn, he got an update on the night's patrols and found that the battle at the Guildhall had quieted the Invictus, at least for the present, and only two patrols reported skirmishes, each squad dispatching the enemy, no survivors.

"Good. That's good. I'll be joining you at full dark, as usual."

"You could take the night off."

"No reason to."

Finn didn't respond.

The Guardsman's silence ticked Ethan off, because he could feel his lieutenant frowning his disapproval yet again. Damn Finn. For the past two years he'd been riding Ethan hard about letting his men do more. But how could Ethan relinquish what had been so solemnly given into his care? The one thing Finn would never understand was what it felt like to be a mastyr vampire, what level of responsibility came with that title.

So, he'd just have to suck it up. "See you at nightfall."

He hung up and set his mind to what items of realm business he needed to attend to. The mayor of Cameron, his realm's largest city, wanted a conference sometime next week about setting up a federation of sister-cities of the Nine Realms. Ethan might be in charge of border security, but the mayors held the cities and towns together, which still didn't eliminate the need for Ethan to have his hand in the day-to-day political machinery of realm-life.

Showering, he recalled what he'd done with Samantha just a few hours ago, how she'd lathered him and he'd returned the favor, the intense love-making, the unexpected depth of connection because of shared frequencies.

Sweet Goddess, he'd like to do that again.

But as he toweled off and started blowing the mass of his hair dry, he scowled at his reflection. What the hell was he doing with Samantha, anyway? Yes, her blood had stopped what had been decades of blood-starvation and he would always be grateful, but beyond that, she was a half-human who didn't want to be here and he had no interest in a long-term anything.

He also knew that if he didn't take steps to create some kind of tolerable distance from her, things could get messy. She might get attached to him in a way he couldn't reciprocate.

He had to figure some way to keep her safe and get rid of her at the same time.

It dawned on him that his other fae guest, Vojalie, might hold the key for him and his chest expanded as a full-blown concept came to him that would answer all his problems and be a good thing for Samantha at the same time.

*** *** ***

Samantha held the fresh, sliced strawberries to her lips, carried there by a fork, and stared at Ethan. "Say, what?" Had she heard him right. She let the strawberries slide into her mouth then chewed, but she'd lost the ability to taste what had begun as a promising bowl of ripe fruit.

"It would only be temporary." He scowled, then crossed his arms over his chest. He stood next to the table opposite her, having arrived with a clear purpose in mind.

Davido sat beside Samantha, holding baby Bernice over his left shoulder, rubbing her back in slow circles.

Vojalie was at the long table as well. She'd been nursing the baby and was waiting for a burp before continuing. She had a flannel shawl, in a soft shade of lavender, draped over her shoulder to her waist. She was a mother with practice. She glanced slowly from Samantha to Ethan, her large brown eyes wide.

Samantha drew a deep breath and addressed the subject straight out. "Ethan, I don't know what bug crawled up your butt, but the last thing I'm going to do is leaving Bergisson for Merhaine Realm. Even I, in just the infancy of my powers, know I belong here."

"You're going. The Mastyr of Merhaine, Gerrod, is already bonded to his woman, Abigail, so I won't have to worry about him going after you. Vojalie can teach you from her home as well as any other place. And right now, I need to focus on Ry and his current leadership of the Invictus. We could be attacked at any moment and I need you safe."

"You need me out of the way." She set her fork down and leaned back in her chair. She'd finished half her breakfast, but had suddenly lost her appetite for the rest.

She watched Ethan beneath hooded lids, his aggressive stance, the set of his chin, his biceps flexing then releasing.

She'd felt those arms last night, same reflexes, different situation.

When she'd awakened and seen just how deeply he slept, she'd left his bed, returned to her room, and dressed for the day. But the entire time, butterflies had flitted around her stomach as she wondered what Ethan would think of the night they'd spent together, whether he'd in any way felt as altered this morning as she did, and somehow hoping that his first words would be as full of awe as she felt.

She couldn't have been more mistaken, since after an initial greeting upon approaching the table, he'd said, 'I'm sending you to Merhaine.'

"I'm not going. I'm staying here. I belong here. I feel it in every fae-ish vibration through my body right now."

Ethan shifted to Vojalie. "Back me up on this, would you?"

Vojalie held his gaze steadily. "I refuse to support either of you. There's an awful lot of belligerence on both sides. No, you'll have to resolve this one yourselves."

Ethan's scowl deepened as he turned the force of his gaze back on Samantha. "Look. I have a lot of responsibilities and going to Merhaine makes things simpler."

"For you, yes, but I have a stake in what happens here as well and I insist on staying in Bergisson. In fact, I'll go back to Shreveport before I get packed off to another realm."

"Shreveport," he all but shouted. "The hell you will."

"Don't you see that this isn't a simple situation?"

"I see clearly enough to know that Merhaine is the right course and I won't be moved on this point."

Samantha glanced at Vojalie who merely shrugged as if to say 'good luck'. But Samantha actually agreed with her, that she and Ethan needed to work this one out.

As if on cue, Bernice belched.

Davido laughed and murmured against the baby's cheek. "I was thinking the same thing, my most beautiful darling." Bernice kicked her legs and cooed.

For a moment, Ethan's scowl eased and his lips quirked but soon enough he had his 'mastyr's' demeanor under control once more.

Samantha glanced at Davido, who winked at her. He kissed Bernice's sweet baby-curls but said nothing. There was however a sense of goodness and wisdom, very ancient wisdom in his eyes. Though she had no way of knowing or proving the sudden intuition that came to her, but she felt certain Davido was over two thousand years old.

She felt something else as well, a soft vibration deep in the center of her faeness and the vibration went on and on. Had Davido rung that bell?

She glanced back at Ethan. He had his warrior's face on and arguing would be pointless. Typical stubborn male.

But she had her own profound level of obstinacy, something that had more than once ended a fairly decent relationship. Maybe she should try a different tack, something more centered on the realm-world than her human experience.

She took a deep breath and closed her eyes. Focusing on the fae part of her still vibrating softly, perhaps thanks to Davido, she let all that power flow to the surface of her being.

Her neck arched as she grabbed a lung-full of air. The resulting flow of energy surprised her since it was so much stronger than the previous night, as though while she slept, she'd been growing her power.

And she knew what would follow as images began to creep through her mind.

When the vision arrived in full, she opened her eyes, but she no longer saw Ethan's dining room, or anyone with her.

Instead, a mastyr vampire appeared, with black hair that flowed away from his face in thick waves, yet very different from Ry. His eyes were large and fierce beneath thick black brows. His nose had a strange curve. Maybe it had been broken at one time and not healed properly. His lips were thick and sensual. He was gorgeous and wild-looking, almost maniacal.

He flew over a tall rise of rock, almost a monolith. She felt something from the rock, something that wasn't rock, but had the properties of minerals, which seemed to call to her. Crystals. Lots of blue crystals.

But the vampire caught her attention since he flew directly at her, wielding a short sword, a weapon larger than a dagger.

She realized she hovered in the air and when she looked down, she saw a gully of some kind, though very deep and equally wide. A gorge, maybe. A dry stream bed ran through the middle and she had two impressions: That something wonderful had happened here and something horrible, a great tragedy, in fact.

The vision pulled her off to the side, to the tree-laden ridges above the gorge where Invictus wraith-pairs and Guardsmen battled fiercely.

Ry was there as well, and something else, something that grew instantly blurred and suddenly the images started to slip away and the vision faded.

She tried to call it back, to learn what happened to the dark warrior, to Ethan, to his Guard, even to Ry, but nothing came to her.

She blinked several times and found everyone staring at her including Bernice who looked surprised. A surprised baby. She stretched, or seemed to stretch, a hand out to Samantha, who took the three-month-old easily in her arms. She was incredibly light and felt like heaven in her arms. She met Vojalie's gaze. The woman had tears in her eyes.

"Another vision?" Vojalie asked.

"Yes, but what does that have to do with Bernice?" Samantha stared down into the infant's contented face.

"She's sensitive to faeness."

Davido patted Samantha's shoulder.

"Of course she would be." And the strangest sense of *family* moved through her, that in some inexplicable way, Bernice belonged to her. She'd felt something similar with Vojalie at the Guildhall, that what she'd come to in Bergisson had been built into her genetic code, another indication, no doubt, of her faeness.

Her gaze traveled to Ethan who stared at her with something like amazement. *I felt what you experienced, even though I couldn't see anything. I felt your shock, your wonder, and your sudden concern and fear.*

She nodded. "Should I tell everyone about the vision? It involves you and a place that looks like a gorge."

His brows rose. "A gorge?" He released a heavy breath. "Yes, I trust Davido and Vojalie implicitly. What did you see?"

She retold the vision in great detail, adding as much as came to her including the pines on the facing ridges, the shrubs, the dry streambed, the monolith to the east, the way the gorge felt tragic.

She didn't look at any of them until she finished recounting what she'd seen. So, it came as a shock to her that both Davido and Vojalie were looking at Ethan, who in turn pulled the chair out across from Samantha and sat down.

Because she could sense his frequency, she could also feel what he was feeling. What returned to her though was more a sense of grief than anything else.

He stared at the table, his left forearm settled in front of him.

She'd made some kind of mistake, but she had no idea what it was. "Ethan, what's wrong?"

He met her gaze, but his eyes had a hollowed out look like he'd been battered by her words. "I have no doubt, not one, that you've described Sweet Gorge, where my family died forty years ago. And now you've had a vision of a forthcoming battle at the same location."

"Oh, God, I'm so sorry. If I'd had even the smallest idea, I wouldn't have just barreled into it like that. I apologize."

"You don't need to, yet somehow knowing that the future will take me back there, against Ry, has brought the former memories returning."

"You mean what you experienced all those years ago?"

He nodded.

She felt the depth of his grief then, like a burden that lived in his soul, a constant weight of guilt that he could never quite release. "You believe you could have done something to prevent the massacre."

"I should have been there." He laughed bitterly. "But I went to the beach in Grochaire Realm, partying with Quinlan, who is mastyr there, the one you just described, by the way. I should have been at the gorge with my sister and my parents. I could have saved them."

"And that is the lie you tell yourself that must change." Davido's voice rang through the room, startling Bernice who had fallen asleep on Samantha's shoulder.

Samantha gentled the baby with her hand on her back and the child released a sigh and fell back asleep.

"It's not a lie." Ethan stated, more quietly, for the baby's sake.

"There were a hundred Invictus that night and you would have been the only Guardsman on the ground. You would have died with all the others."

"If I'd stayed here, where I belonged, then there would have been no such attack."

"You can't know that, Ethan, and you torture yourself with unknowns. You've robbed yourself of a meaningful life trying to make certain something bad doesn't happen again. But you've curtailed the growth of others as well by not expanding your rule properly because of it."

"Bullshit. I've saved lives."

"Of course you have. That's not the point. I'm talking about you and your life, about increasing the responsibilities of those around you who are worthy of greater command. Then, you could enjoy a broader sort of existence. Maybe even have a girlfriend."

Samantha wanted Davido to back off. She didn't know why he was biting at Ethan's heels, so she decided to intrude. "Easy for you to say, Davido. You're not a warrior."

He turned to her, his brows lifted in surprise just as his baby's had been earlier. "There you have me."

"Exactly. I'm a jewelry designer, but even I know better than to try to discipline an accountant or a waitress on how to improve job performance."

"Well, well," his light eyes twinkled. "You have some serious chops, don't you?" Before she could respond, he turned to Ethan.

"Do you agree with Samantha? Has a mere mortal troll been trying to discipline a warrior?"

Ethan shook his head, but he chuckled. "I'm beginning to think that our Samantha will leave none of us alone."

"That's not a bad thing and maybe she's arrived in your life to open your path up. But unlike my wife, I'm going to take sides. I'm with Samantha. She needs to stay in Bergisson and you need to keep guard over her. Let Finn take the lead for a few nights. You've been training him for decades. He's a capable leader and he knows what to do."

Ethan looked thoughtful. Samantha knew he was processing the vision, Davido's advice, and her own refusal to budge.

Finally, he met her gaze. "So, you want to stay here?"

"Yes, and hopefully Vojalie will remain as well." She turned toward her. "I need to learn from you so I can make the best decisions. Are you willing to teach me about my heritage and my gifts?"

Vojalie smiled and nodded. "I'll stay here as long as you need me."

Ethan leaned back in his chair, addressing Vojalie. "And do you truly think this is the best course as well?"

"I think the Guildhall will have as many advantages as my own studio in Merhaine. And should Samantha decide at some point to make her home in the realm-world, I would like her to know the Fae Guild inside and out.

"However, I do agree with my husband on one point: You should stick close to her, Ethan, at least tonight. Samantha is just gaining her power and will need your protection, especially from Ry, but not just from him.

"There is an ancient fae power at large, something that I've avoided addressing for the past several years because I haven't known what to do about this entity. But the recent intermittent difficulty with the realm-to-realm communications, as well as the increased Invictus activity and unusual organized strategies, have led me to believe that we have a rogue fae of power at work, more than I can measure, operating against the Nine Realms.

"This person, who feels to me like a woman, would have reason to want Samantha either out of the way or aligned with her. Ry has made his allegiances and his purposes clear. You would do well to be Samantha's bodyguard for the time being."

"You truly believe all these things?" Ethan's eyes narrowed as he drew a deep breath.

"Yes, I do."

"Why haven't you spoken sooner? Gerrod mentioned her shortly after Abigail emerged as his blood rose, yet you said nothing."

"The timing didn't feel right."

"And now it does?"

Vojalie nodded.

Ethan turned to Samantha. "I didn't consider your point-of-view here, and I apologize for that. I wanted you safe so I could pursue Ry, but I can see now that the situation isn't simple. I'll do as Vojalie has suggested, I'll stick close and be your bodyguard. So, what would you like to do tonight?"

Samantha smiled. "I want to explore the Guildhall."

"Then we'll do that. In the meantime, I'll give Mastyr Quinlan a shout. Apparently he needs to get his ass over here since we have a battle building at Sweet Gorge."

Chapter Six

Ethan watched Samantha gently hand baby Bernice back to Davido. She then excused herself to change her clothes. Vojalie had recommended loose clothing, something all the fae women wore. He knew it was more than a fashion statement, that something about fae-ness and its related powers functioned better when the women were unrestricted, say, by a tight pair of jeans.

For himself, he liked the jeans Samantha wore and his gaze followed her as she left the room. He couldn't deny the attraction he felt toward her, an almost constant call on his body.

"She is quite beautiful, almost as lovely as my dearest one." David's voice held a hint of amusement.

Ethan shook his head as he rose from the table. "I'm trying not to think about it."

Davido merely chuckled in response.

Thanking Vojalie again for her willingness to stay, he then headed to his office and made the call to Grochaire Realm. Fortunately, this time, realm-to-realm communication worked.

Quinlan's bass voice hit his ear. "Ethan. What the fuck do you want?"

"You're still such a complete ass."

"And you're still a pain in mine. I see you've stayed alive somehow."

"Still kicking."

"Can't talk right now. I've got a *doneuse* with me and we're a little busy."

"You don't sound busy." He smiled though.

Ethan heard a drag on a cigarette. "Just taking a break. In that sense your timing was good. I've got a great view and I'm enjoying it. " A faint moaning in the background confirmed Ethan's suspicion. Quinlan still took his donors to bed and by now Ethan knew exactly what was going on.

A vibration went straight through him as thoughts of Samantha slipped through his head.

He rubbed the back of his neck, squeezed his eyes shut and forced himself to focus. "I won't keep you long. One of the fae had a vision of you, in a battle over Sweet Gorge. How soon can you get your ass over here?"

"Hold on."

Ethan heard murmurs in the background, as Quinlan talked things over with his *doneuse*. Ethan could have extended his hearing to listen to the conversation, but he respected Quinlan's privacy.

Back on the phone, Quinlan said. "Sorry about that. Just needed to figure a couple of things out. Tell me the rest, more about this fae. Do you trust the vision?"

Ethan thought he should just come out with it. "This one's half-fae and half-human."

"That's a lot of power for a partial-fae to have."

He took a deep breath before he said, "Her name is Samantha and she's Andrea's daughter."

"No shit." Quinlan had a deep voice, and it had gone deeper still.

"There's something else. Something you need to know. She's a blood rose."

A slight pause, then, "Are you fucking kidding me? A second one in only a few months? What the hell's going on?"

"So you didn't know. Apparently, it's all over the Bergisson blogs."

Quinlan laughed low. "Again, I've been a little busy."

Ethan strove once more to clear his mind of the suggestive images. He chose to press on. "I'm thinking her arrival might be a reaction to the Invictus, that we've got some kind of rogue fae power on the loose of tremendous ability, who's been working to increase Invictus cohesion."

"Action, reaction."

"Something like that. And Ry's joined up with them. He led a concerted attack at the fairgrounds last night."

A soft hiss sounded and afterward another drag. "That prick. But the hell if I'm surprised."

"He went after Samantha last night. If he'd gotten to her before me, he would have enslaved her."

"Sweet Goddess."

"You said it."

"Okay, so what am I doing in this vision?"

"Fighting for the cause. You're in flight and carrying a short-sword. Lots of Invictus."

"Okay. That's all I need to know. I'll come to you as soon as I see my lieutenants. Just one question: Have you taken from this blood rose? Gerrod said the result is incredible. How's the starvation, right now, I mean?"

Ethan took in a long, slow breath. He searched for even the smallest sensation, a trickle of blood hunger, but found nothing. "It's like it never existed."

"Fuck. Me."

The thought streaked through Ethan's head that he shouldn't let Quinlan get anywhere near Samantha. He knew how he'd reacted to Abigail so he shared with Quinlan what that had been like for him. "You'll want this blood rose really bad. But for now, she's mine. Keep your fucking hands off."

He'd meant to say the whole thing in more diplomatic terms, but even the thought of another mastyr getting near Samantha, caused his fists to ball up and his biceps to twitch. "I need you to understand."

Quinlan chuckled, a low deep sound. "I'm feeling you, Ethan. I'll keep my distance."

"Thank you. So when can you come?"

"I have some things to straighten out with my lieutenants. Three, four hours tops. And if I'm going to stay a few nights, you'll probably want to alert a couple of your *doneuses* that I might need them."

"You got it."

"Around eleven, then?"

"Sounds good."

Ethan ended the call and reached Finn through his telepathic frequency and asked him to stay on point. Finn was all too happy to take charge, eager even, which made Ethan wonder if Davido might be right after all. Maybe he should let go of some of his leadership roles.

But the thought of it, of relinquishing even a small part of his committed rule over Bergisson, sent a flash of guilt through his brain. He'd let down just once, to party with Quinlan, and his family had died.

No, the present circumstances with Samantha were temporary. As soon as he figured out what to do with her, he'd take back the reins.

When Samantha returned, however, wearing a loose, red-flowered dress to mid-calf, his heart paused in his chest. She was so beautiful and walked with willowy ease. Hell, even beyond her blood rose qualities, he was drawn to her.

So exactly how easy was it going to be to let her go?

*** *** ***

Samantha's heart pounded and not just because she was in flight, or because Ethan's heavily muscled arms surrounded her, or his tough, wild, grassy scent teased her senses. Nor was it a blood rose thing, although that existed as well, an acute awareness of Ethan's feeding requirements like a temperature she could take by just thinking the thought.

No, the excitement she felt was all about her heritage, her faeness, and discovering what powers she possessed beyond her visions of the future.

She'd seen Vojalie's expression when Samantha had come out of the vision, something approaching a deep sense of hope. The realm-world needed Samantha; she felt it in her bones.

She sighed as Ethan moved swiftly along the deep oak wood path that would eventually lead to the Guildhall. This middle portion of his realm appeared to be mostly wooded with numerous lakes and streams. She'd already learned that Sweet Gorge, the place in her vision, had once had a good-sized stream running through that met up with Bergisson River, the main water source for the realm.

But after the terrible Invictus massacre that had stripped Ethan of his family, the stream had mysteriously dried up. No one, in any of the Nine Realms, understood the cause, though the most powerful of the fae, like Vojalie, had detected an ancient fae magic at the top of the now-non-existent waterfall, near the eastern monolith of the gorge.

Vojalie had shared some of her thoughts before leaving Ethan's house, that she had for a long time believed that an unknown, but very powerful fae had magically dammed up the stream and turned what used to be a lush resort into an abandoned, overgrown, weedy hollow.

As Samantha mulled this over, something within her faeness knew Vojalie was right and now it would seem that the increase in Invictus pairs and the strange disappearance of the stream might just be connected.

Each time Samantha thought of the recent vision that involved Sweet Gorge, she had a strong prescience that something critical would soon take place there and that she would have a role to play as well.

She shivered slightly as she considered the possibility of being more and more involved in Bergisson.

You okay? Ethan pathed.

You could sense that?

She felt him sigh as he shifted to fly around an old tree stump. *My frequency is tuned into you now. It's hard not to know what you're feeling one minute out of two.*

She could feel his distress as well, his concern for her and his ever-present anxiety about Bergisson. *I know what you mean. I'll try to calm my thoughts for now.*

Probably a good idea.

She did just that, and gave herself to the phenomenal experience of flying through his realm, held so firmly within his arms, and moving at a swift pace through a variety of terrain from woodland, to pasture, from hamlet to town. Crossing Bergisson river sent a cool sweep of moist air flowing over her, which felt wonderful.

Finally, the Guildhall grounds, from the day before, came into view. Today, all the tents were gone and only a handful of cars dotted the parking lot.

He moved slower on descent.

The female figure, on top of the highest building dome, moved slightly with the breeze, the metal wings free to swing back and forth.

As he flew her to the double-arched doors, standing wide with lights mounted on either side, several women entered the building.

I'm glad you're with me, she pathed.

I am, too. I'm feeling what you're feeling, that the Guildhall has meaning to you and that I should be with you as well. This was the right choice. I didn't mean to seem so harsh earlier.

Well, I'm sure that won't be the first bump we encounter.

He chuckled softly, a good sign, as he touched down and brought her onto the light-colored pavers in front of the doorway.

Though she'd been in the building briefly the night before, she hadn't explored the depths of the building, which she understood contained a variety of rooms meant only for fae use.

When the Invictus had attacked, the realm-folk had filed quickly and quietly, by long habit, into a vast underground system that had several secret, guarded exits well over a half mile distant in some places. Vojalie had told her that if necessary, she and several of the fae, could have gotten everyone to safety. But they were reluctant to expose these tunnels because of the Invictus and the possibility of traitors like Ry.

Vojalie, who had gone on ahead by just a few minutes to arrange the use of the central domed room, waved a greeting at the top of a short flight of carpeted stairs. The building was very quiet.

As Samantha mounted the stairs, she became acutely aware of Ethan, that he stood right behind her, very close, one hand on her hip. She felt his possessive need of her like waves of heat pouring off sun-drenched rocks.

She looked up at him and he met and held her gaze. *It's always there, this desire between us, this need.*

He smiled ruefully. *Yeah, it is.*

His personal frequency reached for her and sent fingers touching places within her own fae frequency that ignited a sudden desire of her own. He didn't try to communicate telepathically and in this moment anything verbal wasn't necessary at all.

In so many ways, her situation with Ethan, with being a blood rose and a powerful fae, had complicated her life in ways she was just beginning to understand.

*** *** ***

Ethan had been in the fae-guild many times, especially the main banqueting hall for their annual dinners. But he could count on one hand the times he'd been upstairs, the place the powerful fae of his realm gathered to restore themselves, to refresh their power, to discover new abilities.

As Mastyr of Bergisson, he could go anywhere he liked. No door was closed to him, including the central meeting room, which the fae treated with deep respect. Both he and Samantha moved around the space, though in opposite directions.

The holiest of holies traveled in a circle around a central domed ceiling. In the center of that dome another portion of the ceiling rose an additional twenty feet, which made up the minaret, visible from outside.

What couldn't be seen clearly, unless a person flew directly overhead, was the roof of the minaret, on which the winged woman stood. Thick, clear crystal, in an intricate pattern, constructed this portion of the Guildhall, visible only from inside the room.

Vojalie had once told him that great power could come from the right fae standing beneath all that crystal. But even she didn't possess that kind of power. Whether Andrea, with abilities acknowledged to match Vojalie's, could have accessed the power of the crystal would never be known since Andrea had refused testing repeatedly.

Vojalie said that during the day the sunlight shone in a kaleidoscope pattern, shifting as the sun moved overhead. At night, given the lit wall sconces that surrounded the large circular area, no patterns emerged. He imagined only during a very bright moon, at exactly the right angle, significant designs would emerge, and only then if all the lights were out.

"Ethan?" She called to him from across the room. Vojalie stood near the central circle.

He turned toward Samantha, who smiled as she held her hand out to him. He moved toward her as though by a familiar path that his feet had known for centuries. He took her extended hand. "What is it? Everything okay?"

"Yes, of course. Vojalie said you could do this with me. She even thought I might need your help."

He glanced up at the crystal ceiling. "She wants you tested? Right now?"

"Yes. Do you have a problem with that?"

He shook his head slowly. "No, I suppose not." Vojalie was in charge of this part of the show, but his reticence came from the significance of the test.

He crossed with her, heading toward Vojalie and stepping down into a second circular tiled area in the center of the room, sunken by about a half foot.

Vojalie's eyes were bright, expectant. He realized suddenly that the fae leader held high hopes for Samantha, but he wasn't sure she understood the level of Samantha's resistance to remaining in the Nine Realms.

The area was about fifteen feet in diameter, not a large space, and laid out in two shades of tile, all sustaining the circular pattern. In the very center, was a smaller circle of red tile about three feet across. A rough, gray stone pillar sat off to the side and held some sort of shallow stone bowl.

At first, he thought Vojalie would add water, a sort of purification ceremony. Instead, she added several twigs and using a long match, struck on the side of the stone, lit them.

A bitter scent, like oak leaves burning, permeated the space.

Samantha, apparently sensing something, moved close and using her cupped hands, brought the smoke toward her. Slowly her neck arched. Vojalie appeared solemn and gestured for Ethan to get close to the stone bowl as well.

The fragrance eased him, but as he glanced at Samantha, he saw ecstasy on her face as she breathed in the ancient scent.

"How could my mother have ever left Bergisson and all these experiences? I feel connected to the Guildhall as though the community pulses in every beat of my heart." She opened her eyes and glanced from him to Vojalie, then back. "I can feel you both, your strength, your confidence, your boldness. You're very much alike."

He met Vojalie's smiling eyes. "I always suspected as much," he said. "You've got a warrior's heart."

Vojalie nodded. "I fight for the realm-world, just like you, but not with a blade or the palm-energy you can create."

Samantha addressed Vojalie. "Why did my mother leave? I mean, what did you see from your perspective?"

Vojalie appeared suddenly very sad. "The death of her husband took a toll and she became increasingly unsettled, beyond the effects of her grief. There were times I even thought…" but she broke off, her fingers pressed to her lips.

"What?" Ethan asked.

Vojalie took several shallow breaths as though struggling with what she wanted to say. "I've never said this to anyone, but recently I've begun to wonder if some force interfered with her."

"You mean like this rogue fae entity that seems to be present, but which we can't pin down?"

Vojalie met and held Ethan's gaze. "Yes, that's what I've thought, for a very long time. What if the same magic that has ruined Sweet Gorge also got to Andrea, pushing her out of Bergisson?"

Ethan felt as though he'd been struck hard. His chin even lifted, arching his neck, as though he'd taken a blow. "But that would mean she wouldn't have been responsible for what happened at the gorge forty years ago?"

Vojalie's complexion turned pink as her anger rushed at him like a hot wind. "A fae who has a vision cannot be held responsible for what happens in the future. You've blamed Andrea these past four decades, and you were wrong to do so."

Ethan scowled. "She saw a vision of the massacre at the gorge, but instead of letting me know, or anyone else who could have made a difference, she packed her bags and stole off illegally to Shreveport. My family died that night and one word of warning from Andrea could have saved them." A cold, bitter sensation worked within his heart, burrowing deep. If Andrea were here today, he'd accuse her of misconduct and he'd see her tried in one of the fae-courts.

Of course, he would have fought the Fae Guild the entire way, but he never had a chance to bring her to justice. She was gone for ten years before anyone knew she'd settled in Shreveport and remarried. By then it was too late to bring her back; she was under the protection of a foreign government, married to a human.

"You don't know whether she had a vision of the massacre or not. None of us do."

"She communicated with my Guard all the time. We always had warnings from her if something big was going down. Why would this have been any different?"

"You really do blame my mother."

Ethan met her gaze, her unusual, light blue eyes. For just a moment, she wasn't his blood rose, but something else, the daughter of the woman he blamed for the death of his family. And here was another reason why he didn't want to do long-term with her. "I've never said this to Vojalie, but I'm going to say it to both of you now. Quinlan saw Andrea about twenty years ago, when you would have been a child, but by which time it was legal for realm-folk to travel into the access towns, like Shreveport.

"He'd sought her out, having known her even longer than I had. They'd shared meal, and a couple of bottles of wine. She'd broken down and confessed that she could have prevented the attack at Sweet Gorge, that she'd had a vision earlier that day."

Samantha's head shifted back and forth. He felt her disbelief. "But, why didn't she let someone know? What prevented her?"

"No one really knows. Quinlan said she was wracked with guilt, so there you are."

Now Andrea's daughter stood staring at him, a deep frown between her brows, her intense light eyes cloaked with concern and maybe even the despair that her mother had been at fault. "What if I'm the same way? What if I can't take the visions either?

Will you blame me if something goes wrong, if some vision of mine misfires or if I don't report it in time?"

"She's asking the right questions, Ethan." Vojalie had the same worried crease between her brows.

"I already know the answer." He shifted his gaze to Samantha. "No matter what, you have to do your duty, do what's right."

"You're saying my mother didn't."

"Exactly."

"Harsh words, Ethan." Vojalie spoke stridently. "You saw her that last year. She'd lost so much weight. Something was wrong, something beyond our understanding."

"So, you're holding to your theory?"

"All I know is that the woman who left Shreveport didn't resemble the woman I'd known her entire life."

Ethan turned away from both women. Forty years had passed and still the wound bled. He needed to get beyond it, beyond what he'd witnessed that day, but how? And how the hell was he supposed to work with the daughter of the woman he blamed for the deaths of his mother, father and younger sister?

He felt a hand on his shoulder as Samantha's voice entered his mind. *Ethan, I'm sorry for what happened all those years ago, but I can't answer for my mother's sins. However, I can promise that I'll do my best not to let any personal failings I have come between this gift that's emerging in me and the attending duty to help Bergisson. For now, let's focus on my issues because I think there's something here, something that can be of use to you.*

At that, he turned toward her, catching her hand and holding it. "What are you saying? Another vision?"

"Maybe. Ry keeps coming to mind, repeatedly, as though knocking on a door. And I don't mean *him*, I mean thoughts of him. I think I'm supposed to have a vision about him."

"Right now? And what do you mean, you're supposed to have a vision?"

"I can't explain it. I just have this sense that if I were to really let go, I'd be able to see something about him, or about his current activities, maybe even where he's located."

"Is something stopping you?"

"I feel blocked somehow." She turned to Vojalie. "Would this be normal?"

"In every possible way. First, you're just learning to access your vision-based power and second, next to Ethan, Ry is the most powerful vampire in Bergisson Realm. He would have some ability to conceal his activities from the fae, especially if he's able to enlist the help of one of our specie."

"I have a sense of urgency, like I need to find out what's going on. Is there anything we can do to enhance what's happening to me?" She smiled. "Is there an incantation I could use?"

Ethan saw the teasing light in her eye and something within his chest released, a tension he'd been holding. Samantha would need a sense of humor if she chose to stay in Bergisson.

Vojalie chuckled. "No, nothing like that, but do you remember the conversation we had earlier, about the conservatory and hearing sounds like soft, angelic singing?"

"Yes, the first night I slept with the door open. I had such a peaceful night's sleep."

She glanced up at the crystal ceiling. "I think you might be the one to embrace this energy, to harness it. Are you willing to try?"

"Yes."

There was no doubt, no wavering in her response. Ethan valued this about Samantha; the woman had courage.

Vojalie's expression grew serious once more. "I've been waiting a long time to find a fae who could create a connection with the crystal alignments in the ceiling design of the minaret. So let's see what you've got."

Vojalie held out her hand.

*** *** ***

Samantha glanced at Vojalie's smooth pink palm. The fae woman had delicate hands and long fingers, beautiful nails. But she'd also just issued a challenge to Samantha, something she couldn't resist.

Samantha might be an artistic jewelry designer, generally considerate of others, and basically disposed to let life take its own sweet time, but she was also a trifle competitive by nature. So, she slapped her hand in Vojalie's. "Hell, yeah."

Ethan chuckled and put his hand over their joined fingers and gave a squeeze. "I like this. I do. Very warrior-like."

Samantha nodded. "And from what I've seen of Ry, besides the mere fact that he's aligned himself with the Invictus, the bastard deserves to be brought to earth, the sooner the better." She glanced up at the crystal configuration. "So, what do I do?" She then shifted her gaze to Vojalie.

But the fae, as powerful as she was, merely shrugged. "I have no idea. We've all stood in the central red circle, beneath the minaret roof, but nothing much came of it, not for any of us.

"However, you're a blood rose and connected to a powerful mastyr vampire. Maybe this will make the difference. All I can suggest to you is to go with your instincts, follow your call on your faeness."

Samantha turned toward the central circle of tile. As she glanced at the floor, she realized she was looking at blood red pavers made up of crystals. She took a deep breath and moved forward quickly, pulling her hand from Ethan's. This first part of the process she had to do herself, but the moment she stepped onto the round garnet tiles, pieces of the puzzle clicked into place. Her fae vibration became a sudden solid stream within her, a line that ran from her feet through her entire body, flowing up and up.

She gasped, shoulders tensing.

A brilliant flash of light followed.

Then nothing.

She awoke staring into Ethan's concerned, smoky, light brown eyes. He held her hand. "What happened?"

"You passed out."

She blinked, trying to make sense of why she lay off to the side of the crystal pathway. "I felt my faeness like a river through my body."

She turned her head slightly meeting Vojalie's concerned gaze, but a light shone in her eyes as well.

"Did I experience what you've been looking for?"

Vojalie nodded. "I think so, but the power that flowed overwhelmed you."

"Yes, it did. The last thing I remember was a burst of light." She sat up expecting to feel dizzy. Instead, she felt good, really good. Alive.

She gained her feet with the help of both Ethan and Vojalie and before they could stop her, she stepped onto the ruby-red disk again. She wanted more and opened her faeness quickly.

Another explosion of light.

When she opened her eyes this time, Ethan's jaw worked. "Don't do that again."

"I have to. And, it's not bad. It doesn't hurt. In fact, the sensation is wonderful but I'm meant to do this, to connect with my power through the crystal ceiling."

"We know that," Vojalie stated. "But it's clear to me you need support. This time, let Ethan hold you, be a sort of anchor while the power flows. At the very least he can catch you if you pass out again."

Samantha let Ethan lift her to her feet and she nodded. "Are you willing?"

He lifted a brow. "Of course."

Samantha's breath caught and held. She had so many questions about her place in Bergisson and she had questions about where she should land, whether the Nine Realms or Shreveport. But in this moment, she knew one thing for certain: She could rely on Ethan because he said 'of course' without batting an eye, without the smallest hesitation.

This vampire could go the distance. At his most essential, this was his truth.

Moving to the edge of the circle once more, she stared at him, her lips parted.

What is it? His voice in her head startled her, a sensation that soon gave way to pleasure.

You amaze me, Ethan. I've never known anyone like you. I know you'd rather be with Finn and your Guard right now, but instead you're here. And not just here: You're fully present. You're with me.

His brows drew together and he shook his head. *Where else would I be? You need my help, so of course I'd support you.*

That the concept seemed as natural as breathing to him, tightened the very bottom of Samantha's heart. Again, 'go the distance' came to mind.

She turned to face the circle once more.

How would you like me to hold you?

The question made her smile. *Tight, both arms wrapped around me, front-to-front, my arms sliding around your neck as you kiss me.*

He chuckled. *Enough of that or I'll embarrass myself in front of Vojalie and you know exactly what I mean.*

Yes. And I'm hoping we get to do that again soon.

A slight pause, then his voice seemed softer within her mind as he responded, *Me, too.*

He met and held her gaze but no words, telepathically or otherwise, followed. He just looked at her.

Samantha looked back, savoring his smoky gray-brown eyes, the hungry look coming from the depths of him. She could even feel that she would need to donate again. She nodded, wanting him to know that she understood.

He dipped his chin in return.

"Put your arm around my waist, walk me beneath the minaret roof, then hold on. I have a feeling that what will happen will be as sudden as before, maybe even more so because you'll be with me."

"Understood."

He slid his arm quickly around her and without hesitation, she resumed her place. He shifted to stand behind her but enfolded her in his arms. She'd never felt more secure.

As before, her faeness formed a quick river of energy through her body and she connected with the crystals overhead. She waited for the light to consume her, to take her consciousness yet again, but instead, Ethan acted as a ground and the light moved through her and through him.

Power. That was what she felt. A wonderful stream of fae power that she could access, at least so long as Ethan anchored her.

Extraordinary. His single thought slipped through her mind.

I could stay here forever. And here was her truth, that being held in Ethan's muscular arms and at the same time having this power flow, made her want to stay in Bergisson forever.

She couldn't imagine though, to what purpose such power could be put, but right now that wasn't important. The only thing that seemed to matter was feeling Ethan, knowing him, embracing who he was in his world.

Was this just the blood rose part of her talking? Was it her faeness in response to his realm-ness? Or was it him, that he could go the distance, that she'd already made love with him and it had been incredible?

She didn't have answers, none that made any real sense. She'd lived long enough to know that this moment, as amazing as it was, would pass and the cold reality of day-to-day life would return, of waking up grumpy, of PMS, of having a bad hair day. He would become irritable with Finn or his realm-rule and she'd argue with him about why he left his deodorant sitting on the bathroom sink, all those little things that robbed a relationship of its magic and mystery in that thing called life, whether long-lived or not.

So a kind of war waged in her mind, between just enjoying the moment or holding it up for swift examination. Maybe the trick to life was knowing when to do which of the two.

So, she chose in that moment to let the future go and to just savor.

Ethan seemed to know when that happened because his arms tightened. *I need you, Samantha.*

And I need you. More hard truths. She needed him in her life, a man who could go the distance. *But we should step out of this stream. Vojalie will want a report.*

He moved her easily, side-stepping them both off the red disk, but once the flow of crystal-energy stopped, he didn't let her go. Instead, he turned her in his arms and kissed her, a full-blown, tongue-invading kiss that sent her hands sliding over his back, over the buttery leather of his Guardsman coat and beneath his long mass of golden hair. She kissed him back, not caring that Vojalie stood nearby.

She wanted Ethan to know that he wasn't alone in how he felt.

After a moment, he pulled back and looked at her, smoothing a hand over her face, searching her eyes. *What the hell is this between us?*

I don't know. And she didn't, though it felt like *love*. But how could she possibly be in love with a vampire, and one she'd only known for a couple of nights? Yet love was what she felt, flowing through her right now, just as the power of the crystals had poured along her fae pathway.

Vojalie cleared her throat.

Samantha drew back and blinked several times. Only then did she discover that at least a dozen powerful fae women stood in various places throughout the space.

She might have been embarrassed, but the sisterly spirit of the fae rushed toward her, a sensation of communion and excitement. Ethan must have felt it as well, because he stepped back several feet, then yards, as all the women drew near Samantha, Vojalie as well.

Questions flew: 'What did it feel like?' 'Does the power stay with you?' 'What does it mean?'

Vojalie met her gaze. "Did you have the vision of Ry?"

Samantha shook her head. "No, I didn't get there. But I want to try again."

More questions flowed and Samantha took time to answer each one as best she could but mostly she kept saying, 'I don't know'. All the while, her gaze sought Ethan's, but he rarely made eye contact. He seemed distressed, or maybe it was just his overpowering desire for her that she felt.

As she focused for a moment on her suddenly pounding heart, she realized her vampire needed to be fed again.

She was about to suggest they take a break and take care of business, when another vampire, a male, appeared in the doorway opposite from Ethan. The fae all turned and Samantha's heart now pounded heavier than before, recognizing the vampire for who he was: Another starved but powerful mastyr.

Quinlan had arrived.

Her feet were in motion, heading toward him, before she realized she was moving. This new vampire needed her as well, needed to feed. She could sense his blood-starvation like a metallic flavor on her tongue, starvation that needed easing. Now.

He moved in her direction as well, a dark force; dark hair, black eyes, lowered chin, bigger than Ethan, the one in her vision, and coming at her like a freight train.

Then a wind blew past her, but it wasn't a wind.

It was Ethan.

Chapter Seven

Ethan saw red, lots of it, a bright haze over his vision.

He rammed into Quinlan which sent both of them into the air, then into the wall opposite. The building might have shook, he wasn't sure.

He came up lunging and battling, striking Quinlan with his fists then gathering his power into his shoulders and his arms, until his hands sang with killing energy.

Quinlan did the same.

Ethan released by spreading his fingers wide and met Quinlan's battling energy, both streams engaging in the middle so that sparks flew in every direction.

"Ethan, what the fuck are you doing?" Quinlan's deep voice broke through the fireworks, but Ethan's mind had become locked onto the necessity of killing the vampire who'd gone after his woman.

"You need to die," left his mouth.

"Fuck. Sweet Goddess. Vojalie, do something. Get Samantha to intervene."

Ethan, calm down.

Samantha's sudden voice in his head startled Ethan, jarring him for a moment from the energy he kept focused at the enemy.

You need to feed and I'm ready. Ethan come to me. Take from my vein. Take what you need. I want my hands on you, stroking you until you're ready for me. Let me lie down for you, pull you down on me. My vein is ready.

The erotic images began having an effect. He felt confused and his battle energy began to fade. At the same time, the enemy's eased back as well.

That's it. Come to me. I'm here, to your right.

Then he felt Samantha's touch, her hand on his arm, and he shifted his attention to her. He had to get her out of this place, he had to take her to safety, and he had to let her know she was his.

Without looking back, he gathered her in his arms and flew her at a speed he'd never used before. He saw women scatter as he sped through the halls and down the stairs. Once he reached the open doors that led to the fairgrounds, he shot into the night air, Samantha tight in his arms.

He couldn't take her back to his main house. He needed someplace safer, where he could be alone with her. He had a secure cave-dwelling not far from here.

He flew west, Samantha's raspberry wine scent pouring over him. She wrapped her legs around his waist and her arms around his neck. *Ethan, I need you.* Her hips rocked even while he flew.

Oaks gave way to a forest of beech trees.

Skimming over the top, he searched for the opening in the canopy, the only overhead signal to his fortress home. He flew almost straight down, one arm holding Samantha over her back, the other supporting her bottom.

She was his, and Quinlan couldn't have her. No other mastyr would ever have Samantha. She belonged to him. He'd been inside her, branded her with his seed, made her his even if they hadn't completed the joining that would mark her permanently.

Once below the canopy, he flew along a narrow path, one he'd flown thousands of times before. He knew every twist and turn. Finally, he reached the hillside and the house he'd built of more steel and glass that fronted a cavern and grotto he'd created for his own use. Of his several homes, this one was the most secure.

He touched down in front of the door, but never let go of Samantha. He unlocked using a keypad, passed over the threshold, then sealed up his hiding place.

If he'd ever wondered at his purpose in creating a retreat like this for himself, he now understood why.

The chemicals that still raced through his blood, fogged his mind, telling him his woman was in supreme danger. His rational thoughts hung back, shouting at him, but he couldn't hear the words.

Nothing made sense except the woman in his arms.

She looked up at him, stroking his cheek with the backs of her fingers, turning into him and biting his shoulder through his woven shirt. He must have lost his coat when he'd gone after Quinlan.

He carried her down a set of stairs, shifting into levitated flight so that he floated.

I hear a waterfall.

Yes, we're in my grotto. I need your blood.

A soft groan left her lips and this time she bit his muscled arm, then moved upward to sink her teeth into his shoulder once more.

When he reached the waterfall, at the far end of the cavern, he settled her on her feet then stripped her out of her flowered dress. He might have ripped her bra into two pieces, he wasn't sure.

She stuck close as he got rid of his shirt. She helped him remove his boots and battle leathers. He drew her backward, toward the waterfall and sat down on the stone bench so that the warm spring water struck his back. He spread his legs and drew her between them, pulling her close to take a breast in his mouth.

In this position, he plundered both breasts, sucking on her nipples, working each with his hands, plucking with his fingers, riding his tongue over each mound and rigid tip. She held onto his shoulders, her body undulating as she flexed the breast in his mouth, pushing, wanting more. He sucked harder. She cupped the back of his neck.

Take what you need, Ethan. Take all that you need. Everything. My heart pounds for you now, laden with the supply you're after. Let me feed you.

Samantha, he's not for you.

He's not for me. You're for me.

You're mine.

I'm yours.

He left her breasts and rose to his feet, taking her in his arms. He kissed her hard, driving his tongue between parted lips.

She encircled his neck, dropping her arms to embrace his shoulders, then sinking her nails. The sensation worked him, like everything else worked him right now, whether her voice in his head, her body plastered against his, or the soft recesses of her mouth that he drove into again and again.

How do you want my blood? At my neck? Or how about at my groin, or my arm while I nurse on you low?

He groaned hard. *Hold your breath. I want you to experience this while I make you come.*

Experience what?

The water.

She glanced at the waterfall, then at the stone bench. He turned and pivoted the bench to lie underneath the flow of water.

Oh, I see. Genius.

Ready? He didn't need an answer, not really, not when the scent of her sex now permeated the moist, cool air.

He pulled her backward, beneath the waterfall, protecting her from the full force of the water. He then stretched out on his back and beckoned for her to lie on top of him.

She glanced around first. Ferns grew in abundance because of a natural crevice of light high overhead.

Paradise, she murmured.

Because you're here, yes. He met and held her gaze and took her hand, pulling her close. *Now, mount me. Take me inside you.*

She shifted a leg over his hips and looking down, used one of her hands to guide him to her opening. Her back arched as she sank down on his cock.

I've needed this. Her voice in his head rocked his hips and she moaned heavily.

He held her waist, his hips moving to seat himself deep. *Now lean over me, I'm going to shift beneath the waterfall so that it hits you just right.*

She obeyed, a good thing right now given his mood.

He enfolded her in his arms and wondered if anything could feel better than his woman, pressed against him, locked in his embrace.

He shifted down the bench, positioning them both beneath the flow of water, until the waterfall hit her mid-buttocks, which would give her the best feeling.

"Oh, I see what you were getting at." She moaned softly. "That feels so good."

She looked down at him and her hips began to rise and fall. Her mouth opened wider and wider. "That's incredible. All that sensation. And your frequency is pounding me as well."

She was right. His frequency had opened to its fullest breadth, needing to brand her in this way, to reaffirm that while he was with her, she wasn't to service another vampire and definitely not another mastyr vampire. He aimed his frequency, rapid pulses of vibration from his abdomen, directly into her.

She moaned heavily as her own fae frequency responded, meeting his and entwining as they had before, locking into place, pulsing together rhythmically. He gave a cry as pleasure spiked low, tugging at his balls, stroking his cock. He'd never known so much intense sensation before, or need, or desire.

But the various reactions created a new demand. *Give me your neck.* He still didn't speak out loud. He wasn't sure he could. He felt trapped within his possessive nature.

She pushed her hair to one side. He saw her vein pounding and even above the rushing water and the scent of the ferns, her raspberry-wine blood called to him.

With one arm around her shoulders and pinning her in place, while his hips worked her low, he angled his head and struck her neck. She cried out, her well pulling on his cock at the same time. She was close. He could feel it.

He clamped his mouth over her throat where the puncture marks released the elixir he craved and he began to suck.

*** *** ***

Samantha felt caught up in something enormous as Ethan used his warrior strength to drive his cock deep and keep her upper body still at the same time so that he could drink from her. Where his mouth suckled, sparks of pleasure kept sending shivers and chills down her neck, over her breasts, and down her back and sides.

The whole time, the water added a sensual force, pushing her hips constantly against what was so hard inside her, like hands massaging and kneading.

Pleasure upon pleasure rose over her body. From deep in her faeness, she felt his vampire energy pounding against her, not polite this time, not wanting a simple bonding, but a statement of hard fact, that while she was with him, she was his.

She held back though, just as she held her orgasm at bay, wanting all the sensations to last; neck, cock, the waterfall, his energy and hers.

She was sure she moaned, long deep cries, but the waterfall was loud, and his grunts were animal-like. Did he even known he made those noises? Probably not.

Her body writhed over his now. He may have kept her upper torso anchored, but her hips were free to ride him. She rose up and plunged down. The water grazing her bottom was no doubt hitting him on his upper thighs.

He groaned and growled, still sucking fiercely. *Mine*, came to her, penetrating her thoughts. *Mine.*

Yours, she returned.

She breathed hard. *I'm so close.*

But he let go of her neck and drew back to hold her gaze in his vampire-maddened stare.

She planted her hands on either side of his head, still riding him, more fully now, plunging up and down.

You're mine, Samantha. Say it. Say, 'I'm yours, Ethan.' Say it.

He looked maniacal and yet her body responded, loving that he was more vampire-beast than man, growing tighter for him, sliding up and down his column faster and faster. "I'm yours, Ethan. Yours. All yours."

He nodded, a single swift jerk, but he didn't speak. Instead his telepathy once more punched inside her head. *Say it again. I want to hear you say it again, that you belong to me, that your body belongs to me. Say it.*

"My body belongs to you, Ethan." And did it ever. She felt the release barreling toward her, moving fast in the same way his personal frequency battered her faeness. She knew once he broke through, pleasure would flow, but she held tight.

Let me in, he all but shouted inside her mind. *Let me in.*

No. She shook her hair, made damp by the water bouncing off her ass. She smiled as she lifted her chin, her hips rocking. *Never,* she challenged him. She wanted to see more of his beast.

He rose up just a little, lifting his shoulders up off the stone bench. He caught her arms and held her fast. He was so damn strong. His hips took over the ride. He thrust into her hard, using his vampire strength to piston into her, letting her know he intended to have his way.

At the same time, she felt his frequency power ramping up. She panted, her face no more than a few inches from him, his eyes boring into her. *Come for me, Samantha. Come now...*

At the same moment, his frequency broke through and, like a tidal wave, swamped her faeness.

The orgasm that followed rocketed her into a place she'd never been before. She screamed, but couldn't quite hear herself. Pleasure flowed between her legs, but also deep inside the realm-part of her, washing ecstasy through her entire body in sharp waves through her mind, down to her fingertips so that her hands clenched and released the way her body gave over to the orgasm, all the way to her feet.

He kept working her, and maybe because of the way he'd overtaken her fae frequency, the pleasure kept rolling. She could hardly breathe and he was so hard, rubbing the part of her that clenched with infinite sensation.

Her screams turned to punctuated cries as he thrust in deep hard plunges, then he sped up and more pleasure followed, a second orgasm that overtook the first. When had her eyes closed? How could a woman bear so much sensation? Who the fuck cared, give her more!

Look at me.

She opened her eyes and met his gaze. He'd held back until just this moment. She smiled, maybe a little smugly as she said, "Fuck me, Ethan. Fuck me hard and do it now."

The waterfall became a whirling wave of water that went everywhere as Ethan took her into the air, flipped her, then caught her before she landed hard on her back.

He laid her out flat on the bench, then pumped fast, vampire fast, with a speed that stunned her, faster than even the first time. He held court in her fae energy. He watched her and that's when she let her faeness surround him very deep within. She stroked his vampire-ness and his eyes lit up. His breathing grew labored, his hips pummeling hers. Everything slowed as he sped up, as though time warped.

Sensations drove to another pinnacle, different this time as she focused on his release. She dipped her chin, holding his gaze tight. She slid her hand up his neck and touched his mouth, her fingers seeking entrance. He parted his lips and she slid two fingers inside, mirroring his cock.

Oh, shit, Samantha.

He released, a series of powerful thrusts bringing her again. She screamed her final orgasm, watching him as his back arched, as his body writhed, as pleasure overtook his face. He growled and groaned, his hips slowing down yet wringing the last bit of ecstasy from the shared experience, with several deep, hard thrusts.

She breathed heavily as he fell on her chest, worn out and satisfied. She wrapped him up in her arms, or at least as much of the vampire as she could reach, savoring his muscled, warrior's body and letting herself enjoy the extraordinary thing that had just happened.

She smiled up at the craggy rise of rock that led to a slit in the earth above. She could see a star or two winking. She winked back, so deeply satisfied, she didn't want to move. Ever.

Her vampire had gone caveman and she'd loved it.

And here was something she'd definitely never get to experience in the human world, this level of lovemaking combined with power and an internal, inexplicable fae-vampire frequency exchange. Shreveport looked farther and farther away.

She stroked his hair with her hand. The strands were thick, wet and tangled. He had incredible hair, curly in parts, wavy in others, brown overall but with long golden tendrils and curls that gave him a super-sexy appearance.

Words she shouldn't speak came to mind after such an intense coupling: She loved him.

But that was impossible, wasn't it? She hardly knew him. They'd never even sat and exchanged histories or food preferences or whether he liked foreign films or not, although she suspected *not*. She even smiled. No, Ethan was not a foreign film kind of guy.

He lifted up off her, his lids at half-mast. "I felt you chuckling."

"So which do you prefer, French films or Danish?"

"What? Do either of those countries make serious CGI films?"

She smiled. "Just as I thought. I'll have to find a fae-friend to go to the movies with me, or at least to share a Netflix evening."

"Where'd that come from?"

"Oh, I don't know, that I'm feeling so much right now, but don't really have a basis for all the tenderness and good will pouring out of me."

He planted an elbow on the bench, and still buried inside her he rested his head on his fist so he could see her. "I don't know anything about you, but I love being inside you here," he touched her low, gliding a finger down his cock and onto her mons. "But also here." He touched her sternum with the heel of his palm.

"Yes, that's where we're also connected. You forced me deep into my faeness."

His smile was crooked. "You resisted on purpose, just to work me up, didn't you?"

She breathed and sighed. "I did. It was so much fun."

He frowned. "I was so fucking out of control."

"That was partly my fault. As soon as I saw Quinlan, and felt his blood-starvation, I moved toward him because that was my job."

"Don't remind me." He groaned and rubbed a hand possessively over both breasts. He then leaned down and plucked at each nipple with his lips. After a moment, he said, "You've grown solemn. Why?"

"Where is this going? I feel like I'm on a runaway train but the track is all over the place."

"That's a pretty accurate description but let's take this one night at a time. We've just been through two astonishing things, first beneath the minaret crystal and now this."

She smoothed her hand slowly down his cheek. "I want to share your bed again. I mean, I know that I could easily return to the guest suite, but I want to stick close, at least for now. I know that what's happened, just as you said, is pretty astonishing, but I also know that we each have issues to resolve, heavy ones. Like, I have no idea if I should make my home here.

"And as for you, I'm the daughter of the woman you hold responsible for the deaths of your mother, father and sister. Do you honestly believe we could chart a path together?"

He shook his head. "I don't know. I feel lost from one minute to the next. But I do know we should be getting back. I'll need to apologize to Quinlan."

"Then we should go."

She caressed his face again, which led to his lips finding hers. He kissed her for a long time and she let him. She didn't protest or suggest he had obligations to fulfill. He already knew that.

But she felt his desire to stay just as she didn't want to leave, because once they returned to his home, to Quinlan and the ongoing war, to Vojalie and her expectations, this moment would slip into the past. The amazing sensations she'd experienced would be forgotten, sliding away bit by bit, replaced by duties, decisions, and new obstacles to overcome.

So she let him kiss her until once more he was firm inside her and he took her to the pinnacle all over again.

*** *** ***

Ethan watched Samantha dry her hair. She'd gotten dressed, as had he, but he stared at her as though never seeing her before. Trying to mesh his recent Neanderthal behavior with a woman using his blow dryer in a secret grotto cave he'd built for security purposes, proved a hard exercise for his vampire mind.

He didn't like complications and he especially disliked the disruption of his routine, which for fifty years of his life had meant keeping Bergisson Realm safe from the depredations of the Invictus.

And how the hell was he going to face Quinlan, who he'd asked to come to his realm because of Samantha's vision?

Sweet Goddess, he wasn't sure he could make a bigger mess of his life than what existed right now, in this moment.

Worst of all, his deep mating frequency, the one he'd never allowed another woman to touch, had come alive with Samantha and still vibrated with his recent invasion of her faeness. Peel back one more layer, and all he could really think about was getting inside her again, anyway he could.

He turned away, tightening the woven clasp that held his hair back.

"I'm ready." He felt her approach, then her hand on the back of his arm. "You're so serious right now? What's going on?"

"Reality." He walked briskly back toward the front door. He moved fast so that she had to hurry to keep up.

"You're being rude."

"I'm being practical. This shouldn't have happened."

"Ethan, give it a rest, will you? We're not married." She even laughed.

He turned on her. "How can you make light of this? Everything that just happened changes the future, don't you see that?"

"But I knew this would happen. It always does. It's the way of life. You started thinking about work, didn't you?"

He shrugged. "Of course."

"Then let's focus on that. After I stepped into your shower -- and you have the best showers, by the way -- I got to thinking about Ry and his involvement with the Invictus."

Ethan let out a long deep breath. For some reason he'd been so sure that Samantha would want to deepen their relationship, 'take it to the next level', something he'd heard more times than he wanted to remember in the last decade. He didn't have another level, just his dedication to Bergisson and not bringing a woman on board who could get hurt because of who he was as mastyr of his realm. So it eased him that she spoke of Ry and not about love or commitment or anything else.

Ry was also on Ethan's mind; finding him and imprisoning his ass for the next millennium. He also needed to figure out what lay behind the growing organization of the Invictus. They'd never been so disciplined before, fighting as they were now in larger ranks, arrayed like soldiers, trained like fighters. Had Ry done this secretly over the decades, with perhaps the help of this mysterious ancient fae? Or maybe the one called 'the Great Mastyr' was involved as well.

More than anything, he wanted to pull the veil back and have a look at what was there.

When wraiths had first learned to bond with other realm-folk, the ensuing power the newly-created pair could forge, sent them primarily on crime sprees, usually involving draining and killing innocent realm inhabitants. But the last few decades, and especially the last several months, the typical Invictus depredations had turned to objective-based forays, like the one at the Guildhall fair. They seemed to be testing their mettle and improving their battle skills.

Samantha squeezed his arm. "Earlier, before we began exploring the crystal ceiling of the Guildhall, I'd felt a vision wanting to form involving Ry." She smiled and waved a hand to encompass the grotto. "But all this happened. Now I'm thinking maybe we should return to the Guildhall and try it again."

"But I thought you might be too tired."

"Well, I am tired and a little sore in the best way, but exhilarated, too."

"Wait, did I hurt you?"

She purred and moved her hand to rub his chest. "Did it seem like you were hurting me?"

"Well, no, but I was sort of out of control."

"Is that what's really bugging you here?"

He paused for a long moment, searching her light blue eyes, trying to think, to understand. "Yes. I can't afford to be like this. I need you to understand that Bergisson depends on me."

"Okay. So what do you need to do right now then?"

"Contact my men. Finn."

"Then do that. Please, don't wait on me. I'm not a delicate flower that needs to be tended to every second of the day, or rather night." She made a slight gagging sound that forced a smile over his lips.

He leaned into her and taking her face in one hand he kissed her. "Thank you for that. This is new to me and I guess I needed permission."

He felt for his phone then decided on telepathy, partly because of the noise of the waterfall. He opened his pathing frequency, and directed it toward Finn.

Here, Mastyr. Ethan could always count on Finn.

What's it like out there?

Quiet. Too quiet. I have the patrols in the usual places, but there's a vibration in the air.

Ethan shaded his face with his hand. He felt it as well and had ever since the attack at the fairgrounds. Ry would be coming for him, or for Samantha, and if he truly did have command of a new Invictus army, then the whole thing could explode at any moment.

Fine. I'm working things from this end as well, with Samantha. She's got some serious vision-based power. Quinlan's here, too.

That bastard? But even telepathically there was amusement in his voice. *What's he up to?*

The sight of Quinlan going straight for Samantha at the Guildhall flashed through Ethan's mind. For a few painful seconds, he was back there and the Neanderthal need began to rise once more.

Ethan, you there?

Finn's voice snapped him out of the moment and he forced the possessive feelings down as far as he could stuff them. *I'll let you know about Quinlan. I might send him to you.*

That would work. You okay? Ah, shit, I just realized he's a mastyr as well. Did he make a play for your woman?

She's not my woman and yes he did.

Okay, I get it. Stay in touch. Kyle's checking in.

He then called Vojalie and found that she'd returned, as expected, to his primary residence. She was never far from Bernice.

When he mentioned their intention of returning to the Guildhall, Vojalie suggested they try using the conservatory of his primary residence. Since it was clear Samantha had some kind of connection to the crystal patterns in the apex of the roof, he agreed.

"We're heading back to my main house. Vojalie is there now."

"And Quinlan?"

Ethan shuddered as he shook his head. "I need to speak with him, to face him about what happened, but I'll probably be sending him to Finn."

"Sounds good. Ready when you are."

He flew her swiftly back to his home in the southern part of his realm, touching down just outside the door. He took her hand as he walked in, but kept her on his right, placing himself between Samantha and whoever might be in his house.

As it happened, Quinlan sat on the raised fireplace hearth, the baby in his arms.

"Ooooh," Samantha cooed quietly. "How sweet is that? And she looks so tiny in his arms."

Ethan turned his head slowly and glared at Samantha, but her lips quirked which told him she'd been taunting him on purpose. He narrowed his gaze. "Will you behave yourself?"

She caught his woven shirt in her fist and pulled him toward her as she leaned up and planted a full kiss on his lips. "No." She then waved to the inhabitants of the living room.

Panic set in as he followed her. He didn't want another fight, but if she got anywhere near Quinlan, Ethan was pretty sure he'd rip the dark-haired, handsome bastard to shreds.

But when Samantha reached the short set of stairs to the right, she turned back, winked at him, then called out, "Hey, everyone. I'm headed to the conservatory."

Quinlan murmured a greeting but stayed put.

Davido waved at her and said Vojalie was cooking up one of her pasta recipes. "Dinner in a half hour."

"Okay." She disappeared into the hallway.

As Ethan moved the opposite direction, stepping down into the living room, Davido crossed to take Bernice from Quinlan's arms. "I'll just go check on the linguine." He moved swiftly so that within a couple of seconds, Ethan was alone with the vampire who'd trained him both as a Guardsman and how to govern his realm.

Quinlan just shook his head, his hands planted on his hips. "Fuck. So, this is what a blood rose does to a mastyr." His deep voice resonated through the room.

"Welcome to my nightmare. You felt it though, what she was?"

"The moment I saw her, it was as though I recognized her and believe me that was a tornado that drew me in. I didn't have time to think especially when she headed in my direction. Ethan, a thousand apologies."

"This wasn't your fault or hers. Nobody's, except that I'm damn sorry for tackling you."

Quinlan grinned, a rare thing for him. "We'll both have to pay, though, for the damage done to the building. You didn't see it, but we busted a wall up pretty good. There might even be a problem with the joists."

"Well, that's because you're one big motherfucker."

Quinlan laughed but soon grew somber. "I won't be able to stay here. I've dreaded seeing her walk through the door. Sweet Goddess, the smell of her blood! But do you like her, this woman of yours?"

"She's not my woman. Why does everyone have to keep saying that?" Of course remembering the things he'd said to Samantha in the middle of all the recent outrageous sex sort of belied his own constant protestations.

"You didn't answer my question: Do you like her? Is she a decent kind of woman?" He frowned as he asked.

"She…she's not *typical*. But the truth is, I don't know. I barely know her."

"Yet, you trust her. Even I can see that much."

Ethan nodded. He searched around trying to figure out how best to explain what he felt about Samantha, what his deepest frequencies told him about her.

"You know what Davido said?"

Ethan shifted his gaze back to Quinlan. "What?"

"That when she looks at you, she sees you, not just the trappings, but you."

"Yeah, I think she does."

Quinlan elaborated. "It's as though you're suddenly the most important person in the world. She did it just now, to me, when she looked at me."

Ethan bristled, his fists clenching, the muscles of his arms flexing.

But Quinlan laughed. "I'm just jerking your chain, but I will apologize since I can see you're about ready to stroke-out all over again."

Ethan met and held his gaze. "The thing is, if you're around her…"

Quinlan nodded. "I know. So long as you haven't permanently bound her, something Vojalie told me about, then I'll be driven toward her as well.

"So, put me in the field for now. Let me work patrols with Finn, for a night or two. I won't be able to stay away from Grochaire longer than that, but I think I should be here to help settle this thing with Ry and the Invictus he seems to have under his command."

Ethan's first instinct was to send Quinlan back to Grochaire Realm on the double. But that was all about Samantha and not about what was best for Bergisson Realm. He wasn't kidding when he told Samantha that his realm came first.

He nodded. "I agree that I need you here. Work with Finn. He'll know where to fit you in with the current patrol schedule."

*** *** ***

By the time Samantha returned to the main living area, Quinlan had left the house. Without meaning to, she breathed a deep sigh of relief. She held no animosity toward the oversized, handsome vampire, but she was as drawn to him as she was to Ethan, the pull of the mastyr's need hard on her.

Ethan met her at the stairs and explained the situation. "Are you okay?" he asked, his brow wrinkled.

"I'm fine, just trying to find my sea legs."

He turned and gestured with a wave of his hand to the dining area, off the kitchen. "Vojalie has dinner ready. An asparagus cream pasta."

"Sounds wonderful."

"It is. With a nice German wine."

She glanced at him, trying to blend the concepts of vampire, pasta, and wine. Of course she'd grown up knowing about vampires, but she'd always supposed them to be less civilized than this.

A baby-monitor on the table kept the parents relaxed as baby Bernice did her sleeping work.

The conversation was less satisfactory, however, since Ry came up more than once, his defection, and even the possibility that he'd been working with the Invictus for a long time.

Samantha tried not to think about Ry too much, or any of it really, but focused instead on what she needed to do next. The conservatory pulled at her. The songs had spoken to her from the beginning.

"You keep glancing in the direction of the upper quarters?" Vojalie smiled as she spoke, her warm brown eyes glinting. "Are you thinking of the crystal apex?"

"Yes."

"I'm not surprised. I've often thought that with the right fae, the configuration had possibilities."

Samantha turned toward Ethan. "What made you design it that way?"

"I didn't. It was your mother's idea, her design."

"You never told me that?"

Ethan smiled, that big smile of his. "Sorry. But ever since I've met you, I've had a lot of other things occupying my thoughts."

Images of their recent coupling in the grotto flashed through her mind. When he reached for her hand beneath the table, her fingers met his readily and her heart thumped in her chest. "I guess we both have."

He cleared his throat and after giving her fingers a squeeze, he withdrew his hand. "Yes, your mother designed most of the interior of this house. Of course that was before Patrick died. We were very good friends once, even before I became mastyr of Bergisson. "

"Until she left and the disaster happened at Sweet Gorge."

He nodded and set his fork and spoon down. He sat back in his chair. "I wish it were otherwise."

"I wish I understood."

"Understanding will come in its own time," Davido said brightly. "And I want another glass of this excellent wine." He picked the bottle up and refilled his goblet, topping others on request.

After dinner, Vojalie and Davido retired to their suite to tend to Bernice, while Samantha drew Ethan to the conservatory.

She walked in before him, moving slowly and letting the space speak to her. The music came first, a soft humming of the crystals. Ethan had already told her he didn't hear anything, so she felt particularly blessed by the sound.

"I didn't want to try this alone, in case I had a reaction similar to the one at the Guildhall." She reached a hand back for Ethan.

He moved in and took it. "I'm here."

She nodded as she moved toward the center, where the pavers had made a slow, swirling progress to another central disk, directly beneath the apex.

She looked back at him. "Ready?"

He nodded, but there was such tenderness in his eyes that for a moment, her breath caught. This was Ethan, Mastyr of Bergisson, a powerful vampire who could break her with a thought, but he smiled and watched her like she'd become precious to him.

She tried not to make too much of it, but he was so handsome and making love with him had become this incredible, miraculous journey of sensation. She had a fae frequency that he could tap and plunder and which he did willingly.

What are you thinking because I'm reading all sorts of things right now that have nothing to do with fae visions?

Her lips parted and she took a couple of steps backward, reaching the disk then drawing him to her with a pull of her hand. He didn't mistake the invitation, but took her in his arms and kissed her, pressing his body the full length of hers, letting her feel all that he was in the strength of his thighs, his arms, and what grew very firm between them.

She sighed as he kissed her and like magic, her fae power blossomed flowing in a stream upward toward the apex of the crystal ceiling, lighting up, making her feel alive in ways she could never have imagined in her simple student-jewelry-making life in

Shreveport. Was this really her new life, all this power, all this man, and the thundering of her heart that demanded she feed the one holding her in his arms?

He drew back and looked up. "The energy you create feels extraordinary."

"And what amazes me is that I'm not struggling at all, with you holding me, here in your home. That must mean something."

She didn't want to say it, that she belonged here. But Ethan met her gaze and now his smoky gray-brown eyes looked troubled. "Part of me knows, in my gut, we should complete the bonding, to end any chance that Ry can get to you, but I just can't."

"Ethan, what would it involve exactly?"

"What has been explained to me is that when our frequencies are joined, a further act of will is required, a decision to bond by both parties."

"But that's good because then I could never be forced into a bond that I didn't agree to."

His expression grew grim. "You could be forced, you could be worn down, and Ry is just deviant enough to attempt it, one more reason that I need to keep him away from you."

She nodded, the weight of the subject settling in. "But if we were bonded, what then?"

"No one else could get to you. It just wouldn't be physically possible for you to be bonded to two vampires at once, which returns us to the original situation, that I wish I could offer you the protection of a bond right now, but I can't."

She put a hand on his chest. "Don't go there. I couldn't take you up on it even if you offered. I'm not ready and I'm not sure I ever will be."

He nodded, but he looked weighed down again, that sense she had of him, that he'd carried the burden of his world for fifty years, since he'd become mastyr of Bergisson.

Hey, she pathed, giving him a small shake. *Remember what Davido said.*

He nodded, *Understanding comes in its own time.*

This has been like a crash-course in relationships, and I admit, I've never been very good at it.

Well, if you're not very good, then I just plain suck.

She laughed and hugged him. He hugged her back and rocked her as the stream of fae energy flowed with them.

She drew back just enough to hold his forearms, returning to her original purpose in testing out the crystal apex in the first place.

She took a deep breath. "I want to focus on Ry. He's been the problem here, and maybe a vision will come to give us some direction right now."

"Sounds good. Go for it."

Still facing him and holding his arms, she closed her eyes and focused on her faeness as the power continued to stream through her. A vision unfolded, quickly this time, and in a scattering of sudden images telling her all she needed to know.

When she opened her eyes, Ethan stared hard at her. "What have you seen?"

"Ry plans on attacking all the patrols tonight, all at about the same time, a coordinated effort." At the same moment, her head began to hurt and she felt strange, like a different kind of wave had begun pulsing through her mind, something outside her that had nothing to do with her own power.

She looked around and felt as though she were being watched, spied on.

"What is it?"

"I don't know. But I think it might be the ancient fae, the same one at Sweet Gorge."

"Okay." He nodded several times. "Just hold onto me."

"Right." She dipped her chin in response as well. "What will you do?"

"Path Finn."

"Ethan, wait. Before you do, I have this feeling I need to shield you while you do it, to protect your communication."

"Okay."

Chapter Eight

With Samantha's fae power still streaming, Ethan drew her close to his side and nodded to her. He felt her surround him with what he could only describe as a kind of shield or blocking capacity. She was more powerful than he could have ever suspected and he had a strong impulse for that reason alone to keep her with him forever.

But he forced himself to focus instead on the moment, and not on his impulses. With a rogue fae active, even in his own house, even affecting Samantha, and with a disaffected Guardsman who was also a mastyr vampire in league with the Invictus, he knew he was in for it. That Samantha's most recent vision had given him a portal to the future enabling him to warn his battling force, was a huge advantage.

He hugged her as he opened up his telepathy and reached for Finn.

When Ethan told him what was going on, he felt Finn's exasperation. *And that bastard knows our routines, all of them.*

But we've been forewarned. Put everyone on alert, half-swords drawn, attack at will.

Where will you be?

He glanced at Samantha and asked, "Are you sure you saw me in the field? I hate the idea of leaving you right now."

"You were there. I have no doubt about that. You were flying near a tree-line of oaks, I think, maybe not even far from here. But, yes, you were in the field."

He nodded, then to Finn, he pathed, *I'll be with the Guard here.*

Ending the communication, he drew Samantha away from the apex and like water sliding off a slick surface, the power drained away from her. He marveled at all of it.

He took her by the shoulders. "I don't want to go but I won't be far. The oaks are a clue. There are a few groves scattered around my realm, but I can't be far from you right now."

Her smile faltered. "Good. I'm nervous, too." But she drew in a deep breath and added, "I'll walk you to the front door."

By the time Ethan said good-bye, he felt in his bones that leaving Samantha right now was a big mistake. But he had a job to do and the vision had been clear; he'd been with his men, where he should be.

Yet even as he, and six additional Guardsmen, began measured sweeps high in the air over the immense oak grove, his house, and the nearby Guard House training camp, a red wind arrived coming from the east. He alerted one of his Guardsmen to keep watch on all other fronts and the remaining five to form a front battle grid with him against the approaching Invictus wraith-pairs. At the same time, he pathed Finn who said he'd send reinforcements on the double.

As he lined up with his men, he opened his battle frequency and felt his powerful war vibrations attach to each man beside him and down the ranks. Electrical currents pulsed heavily as together they created the fortified energy-shield.

A high-shrieking sound arrived as the Invictus attacked.

And the battle was on.

Energy released from palms, flipped up from wrists. Blue and red streams flew everywhere, striking the energy field and creating small bursts of fireworks, resulting in tears in the field.

At the same time, the Invictus threw blades of different kinds, which hit the web often and sometimes increased those tears, which made sustaining the field even more difficult.

Ethan, as a mastyr vampire, however, had the ability to seal up the breaches and worked his power down the line, both directions. Enough tears, and the Invictus could pass through, which was why, without his support in a battle, one day and with this level of organization and discipline, the Invictus would break apart the field and get through to their goal. A lot of realm-folk would die, including Guardsmen.

The Invictus wraith-pairs could overtake a Guardsman caught alone, the attack savage with physical weapons of all kinds; short-swords, daggers, hatches, spiked ball-and-chains and each pair tended to favor a different kind of weapon.

Ethan's training of his men had become increasingly varied through the years, and especially in recent months.

So basically, before Samantha, he'd worked seven nights a week in order to make sure he was available to sustain the linked battle-shield.

He sent his power now, both directions, mending tears and at times covering a wounded Guardsman to protect him from further injury until he could recover from a quick blow.

But an axe whirred by his head and as he sent another flow of power to seal the resulting breach, something new intruded. From nearby he felt the presence of the dark fae force. Samantha had indicated she was near, but now Ethan felt her vibration as well.

He needed to get this battle over and done with and back to Samantha as soon as possible.

She was in danger.

*** *** ***

Samantha stood at the edge of the conservatory, but didn't quite know how she'd gotten there. She felt oddly dizzy.

All the Guardsmen were outside engaged in a battle she could hear at a distance, so she knew she was safe.

Several lanterns, placed around the lush, crystal enclosed gardens, kept the space in a soft glow, although Samantha's fae vision could have managed the dark easily.

Her legs felt almost fatigued as she moved into the room. Of course, it didn't help that she'd basically switched from days to nights. No wonder she was tired. And her heart was sluggish again. Ethan would require another supply soon, especially because he was battling.

She just felt tired and another wave of dizziness assailed her. Then she felt it, the presence of the ancient fae entity, not far from her now. And as she turned to scan the conservatory, the room began to spin. She didn't understand what was happening to her. She felt very confused.

Suddenly, unexpected images of the previous battle at the Guildhall fairgrounds suddenly burst through her mind, playing one after the other.

She pushed her hands to either side of her head, trying to make the images stop, of Ethan falling, of Guardsmen getting hurt, of the Invictus shrieking as they attacked, of the blue and red streams of light, of a certain acrid, smoky scent in the air.

"Stop," she called out.

"She's had enough." She heard a man's voice, which seemed familiar, but she couldn't quite place it.

Just as quickly, the images slipped away and her mind was once again free.

Samantha opened her eyes. The room no longer spun, but she could see strange waves all around the perimeter. Something was wrong.

Really wrong.

"Samantha?"

She turned slowly, her head muddled and thick. A man stood in front of her now, a vampire, a mastyr vampire.

"Remember me?"

She looked up at him. "Mastyr Ry?" She smelled his blood need and her heart pounded in her chest.

His nostrils flared and his lids lowered to half-mast. "Goddess, your blood smells like heaven."

She knew she shouldn't do it, but she felt compelled as she opened her arms and eased her head to the side, exposing her throat. These were not her arms, her throat, her desires. She knew the dark fae force manipulated her, but she couldn't do anything else.

Ry's fangs emerged, pulling back from his lips. His jaw trembled, then he struck. She felt blissful as he pulled on her vein, drawing sustenance into his starved body. She was fulfilling her most profound purpose in life. But this wasn't Ethan.

Not Ethan. The words left her mind but went nowhere.

She didn't want to feed Ry but she couldn't help herself.

She had to contact Ethan, had to find him.

Ry opened his personal frequency and began pummeling her chest and abdomen trying to get to her faeness. It would take so little to complete the bonding. She understand that now, that it was just a matter of her will, of acquiescing, of saying 'yes', and she'd belong to Ry.

Where was Ethan?

Her mind felt so loose and disjointed. The images of the previous battle at the Guildhall hovered at the edges of her mind, but she forced them away.

She just felt so confused.

Yet she had to do something, she just couldn't remember what? She loved that she was feeding a starved mastyr. But this was Ry, not Ethan.

Ethan. She sent the call out to him as hard as she could, but the communication failed. She felt that the dark fae force had blocked it.

So good to give her blood. More images, though, of the Guildhall battle.

Once more she forced them away.

She had to focus, but on what?

Ethan.

Yet she couldn't reach him.

She relaxed and stopped struggling. Ry's arms tightened around her. At the very least, she wished she was feeding Quinlan instead of Ry.

Quinlan.

Yes, maybe she could reach Quinlan.

Using what was left of her strength as well as what little clarity of mind she had left, she pathed to the Mastyr of Grochaire Realm and found him. *Quinlan, are you there?*

Samantha?

I need help. Ry is here. Can't reach Ethan.

Then her mind once more filled with the horrific visions of the battle at the Guildhall, forced into her mind by the ancient fae.

Ry's voice intruded. "I can stop all these images if you'll just bond with me. Say 'yes', Samantha. Just say 'yes.'"

She wanted to. With all her heart, Samantha wanted the terrible images to stop and Ry sounded so sweet. He was a mastyr and he needed her.

But what about Ethan?

She held on to thoughts of Ethan, then the images looped again, of shrieking and body parts being severed, of enslaved realm-folk dying on the ground.

*** *** ***

Ethan, get over to Samantha now. She's in trouble and she can't reach you.

Quinlan? What the hell's going on? Ethan was in the middle of the battle, sending energy flying in every direction.

Just go! She said something about Ry being there.

Got it! He contacted his Guardsmen, and because they were a well-trained team, the men closed ranks, releasing him from the field.

He felt it now, the same awful presence that he felt at Sweet Gorge, but stronger now, almost thick with energy. And she was in his home.

Sweet Goddess.

He flew straight for his house, going as fast as he could, which meant it only took seconds to reach the front door.

Throwing the door wide, he could sense Samantha now and how close she was to giving herself to Ry. The fae power was intense and where the hell was the Guard he'd left to watch the house?

He found him sunk in stupor just outside the archway to the conservatory, probably enthralled by the ancient fae.

When he moved quickly inside, he saw red all over again. Ry had Samantha in his arms, feeding brutally from her neck, his body hunched over hers.

"Get off my woman!" His voice bellowed through the space, shaking some of the crystal panes but having the good effect of forcing Ry to release Samantha. She was pasty white as she slid to the floor, weak at best, unconscious at worst.

He gathered power into his palms, energy radiating down both arms.

But Ry had just fed on a blood rose, so he turned up his own juice, and with bloodied fangs launched strikes from both palms then threw himself at Ethan.

Power roiled around Ethan, through him, punching at him. But he returned the favor and heard Ry grunt.

A pair of fangs ripped into his left shoulder. He gathered his energy once more and aimed at Ry's back. As soon as he released, Ry shouted his pain, but sent an answering shot at the base of Ethan's spine. He arched away from Ry, rolling in agony, but his enemy had just fed, more powerful than ever before.

Damn, he needed help here.

He was on his hands and knees, glaring at Ry who walked around him sneering, gloating. "Feeling weak, mastyr?" He laughed long and low.

And that's when he felt it, the dark fae energy, muddling his mind.

Ethan, Samantha was in his head. *Come to me. Together. We can do this.*

She sounded so weak.

He understood. From his peripheral, he watched her crawling toward the central disk.

He had to get to her so that she could launch her fae power.

He gathered one last bolt of energy and flung it at Ry. At the exact same moment, he levitated in his half-kneeling state, caught Samantha up and slid her the rest of the way. He could feel the moment she let her fae energy flow and it was like a healing salve through his wrecked body.

He took in a long deep breath.

He heard Ry cursing as a faint female voice called out, *We must go. You fool! You failed to complete the bonding!*

He saw Ry fly through the arched doorway and knew when both he and the fae entity had left his house.

He lifted Samantha to her feet, her energy, supported by the crystal apex, still flowing.

He looked down at her and cupped her chin, kissing her on the lips, a soft expression of his gratitude for what had just happened. *You just saved my life.*

She kissed him back. *And you saved mine, again. He almost had me, Ethan. He was drinking from me, and because the blood rose part of me doesn't differentiate, I was so happy to meet that terrible starvation that all of you suffer from.*

But he played into that, and tried to bond with me. All the while, I forced myself to focus on you, but the dark fae being, or whatever it is, started confusing my mind. She kept showing me battle images from the Guildhall fairgrounds, tormenting me.

He drew her into his arms. *It's over and you've been through hell, again.* Guilt swamped him. He should have been here. He should have gone with his gut. When was he going to learn? And yet, she'd been so certain about the vision, not hesitating at all when she told him where she'd seen him.

Can you move us out of this stream, Samantha? I need to contact my men.

She nodded and eased away from the disk. He sidestepped with her and as before, the energy slid away, no stress or strain. He felt completely restored. Even the wound that Ry had inflicted at the base of his spine no longer hurt.

She planted her hand on his chest. "Call your men."

He nodded and pathed to Finn who gave him an update. The Invictus had attacked every patrol and many were still battling. But Finn said the numbers of wraith-pairs captured was high, all being held in prison for later trials.

Ethan kept Samantha close, but the pull to go back out in the field almost overwhelmed him. Because together Ry and the fae entity had been able to enter his house despite the presence of his Guard, he wasn't willing to jeopardize Samantha again tonight. *I need you on this, Finn.*

He outlined what had happened and Finn responded, *I've got this. I'm in touch with Quinlan. He replaced you at the battle near your house, where the Invictus hit the hardest. I'll let him know what's going on.*

I'll be here tonight.

As it should be.

Ethan forced himself to let the whole thing go, the terrible sensation of anxiety that he should be out in the field himself. He'd left Samantha once tonight and he wasn't doing it again.

After contacting Vojalie and making sure her family was safe, he turned Samantha in the direction of his suite of rooms, which he'd built with extra security. Once inside, he made sure the windows were locked down then he bolted the door.

Samantha admitted her fatigue and he gave her one of his tees to sleep in which went all the way to her knees. She looked fragile and sexy and he responded to both images. But he held himself back.

She needed rest.

She fell asleep almost immediately, so he moved into the living area nearest the bedroom door and from which he had a view of the oak grove beyond a thick pane of bullet proof glass. His vampire vision shifted subtly as it moved through the dark of night, through the trees, the black shadows of trunks and branches, but he saw nothing. Nor did he feel either Ry's presence or the fae entity, as he'd come to think of this ancient woman, as an entity, something different from normal realm-folk.

He stood with his knees apart and his arms locked behind his back, restraining the rage he felt that Ry had almost taken what Ethan had come to believe belonged to him. It was a realm thing, a vampire thing, and a very male thing that he wanted Samantha *in that way,* like something his cave-residing ancestors might have done on principle, hauling a woman to his vampire lair, keeping her, making her his repeatedly until her stomach was swollen with his child.

His body trembled with exactly that kind of need and a matching rage that Ry had attempted to force and to trick Samantha into bonding with him.

Sweet Goddess, a few seconds more and he would have lost her, that's what he understood as he stared out into the night, a breeze whipping the leaves and shadows around. The fae entity would have seen to it, would have confused her, and she would have acquiesced.

He'd almost lost her.

The idea of it sickened him. But how was he going to keep on in this way, without binding himself to her? Yet neither was ready to make that level of commitment. They'd barely known each other two nights.

He didn't know what else he could do except stick close until he found a way to confront Ry and either arrest and imprison him or defeat him in battle for good.

*** *** ***

When Samantha awoke late the next evening, she put a hand to her chest, aware first and foremost of her heavily beating heart.

Ethan.

Ethan? She called to him, knowing he needed to be fed.

I'm coming.

She sat up in bed. She wore his t-shirt, the black fabric soft against her skin, his grassy, hillside scent sweet in her nose. She lifted the bottom of the shirt to her face and breathed deeply as desire swirled.

But right on the heels was the need to offer up a vein, so that when he opened the door to the suite, she held out her arms. "Come and take what you need."

The look on his face, of sudden desire and relief mingled, made it an easy decision to take the shirt off and throw the covers back, baring herself to him.

He cried out, closing the door with his foot once more. He got rid of his jeans and long-sleeved tee in a flurry of movement, arriving beside the bed with his gaze fixed to hers.

Thank you, slid from his mind to hers.

She nodded and glanced down at what was firm. *It's okay. I'm ready. I want this. Take it all and take it now.*

I hadn't thought...I hadn't expected...

The words drifted away because he kissed her and positioned himself between her knees.

But she pathed, *You keep forgetting that I'm a blood rose.*

He groaned heavily, plunging his tongue in and out of her mouth.

This coupling would be swift, only as long as it took for him to plunder her vein, but her body ached for him as well, from deep inside to the tips of her fingers and toes. Her fae frequency ignited at the same time reaching for his frequency.

As he slid his cock inside and began to push, he released his frequency and met hers, entwining.

She cried out. Passion flowed and she writhed beneath his body, pulling at the woven clasp to release his long hair, then losing her fingers in the thick curly strands.

She shifted her head on the pillow to expose her neck. He leaned down and with fangs fully emerged he struck to just the right depth and began long pulls.

His hips moved into her then drew back, only to return with heavy thrusts, arching and pushing each time.

Samantha slid from one extraordinary sensation to the next, to the feel of a warrior's muscled body pulsing over hers, his scent in her nose, his frequency stroking hers, working her up, his cock hitting her just right and setting pleasure on pleasure, to his lips sucking her neck and her vein, drawing from her the supply meant for him, meant for a mastyr, meant for Ethan.

Only for you.

Yes, only for me. Mine, Samantha mine.

Yes. She didn't want anyone else to take her like this, to drink from her as Ry had, powering him to hurt the man she...

Samantha drew in a breath and his drinking slowed.

What is it?

I...that is...nothing. She caressed his back, his shoulders, his arms. *Keep taking from me. I love this so much.* She'd almost said she loved him, but how impossible was that? She'd only known him a handful of days.

Yet with all they'd been through, it seemed so much longer. And because she felt his frequency, that she touched what was so intimate in him, in his realm-world, she felt she knew him better than she'd ever known her human boyfriends in the past.

But what did it mean to 'love' Ethan? What could it mean? She would have to give up her life in Shreveport and she wasn't ready to do that. She'd have to become fully 'realm' and she wasn't ready to do that either.

He left her vein and with blood on his lips he looked down at her and caressed her face with his hands. "Where did you go? You were right with me. I want you back."

She nodded. "I want to be back." The movement of his hips had slowed but he still pushed into her and pulled back, in and out. He felt so good and the connection was extraordinary. She wanted more, more of him, more of all that they could be together. She wanted him entangled as he was right this minute with her fae frequency.

She leaned up and grabbed his neck pulling him down to her. "Fuck me, Ethan. You're what I want right now, right this minute. I'm here."

He growled softly and held her gaze as he began to push inside her, heavy thrusts once more hitting her just right so that she began to clench. She could hardly breathe.

"That's it. That's what I wanted. To see you like this, your lips parted."

He drew close and rimmed her lips with his tongue then pistoned his hips and kissed her hard at the same time.

Crying out against his mouth, she came, pleasure rising to a sharp crescendo, streaking through her body, up her abdomen and tightening her fae frequency to join in more pleasure so that she arched her neck and she screamed.

He pistoned hard, his cock ready. He shouted as he came, which brought her again, another flare of sensation that caused her body to writhe beneath his, her hands gripping his muscled arms, her well tightening around him, making him twist over her as the last of his pleasure flowed.

She breathed hard as he eased down on her and as her own body let go and relaxed into the bed.

Perfection.

Couldn't agree more.

He was breathing hard as well.

She surrounded him with her arms. Even their joined frequencies had relaxed but remained connected. She loved this, all of it, the giving of her blood, their frequencies joined, and sex with Ethan.

She didn't want to give this up, but how far would she need to go from all her previous heartfelt plans and dreams, to stay here with him? She didn't know if she could do it, not deep in her heart.

The superficial part, the simple desire to keep making love with him, understood exactly what she should do.

But she was old enough to understand that relationships were anything if not complicated, that pure desire, of any kind, couldn't cut it for the long haul. And by everything she'd seen in the world of the Nine Realms, life would become increasingly complex, not less so were she to fully embrace her fae-self.

"You're thinking hard." His voice came out muffled, pressed as he was against the side of her head. She felt his lips kissing her hair.

"I woke up with a lot on my mind. So tell me about Bergisson, why you love it here."

He took her on a journey of his childhood and how for the first fifteen years of his life, he'd explored every cranny of his world, every mountain and vale, every river, even the oceans between the realm, a world apart from earth, just somehow conjoined.

He spoke of traveling the next fifteen years from realm-to-realm, of meeting each of the mastyrs and knowing from an early age that he would one day be a mastyr and possibly rule a realm, but he'd never really believed it. Ry had ruled Bergisson for a long time. No one could be more powerful than Ry, but so Ethan had proved.

He stayed with her in bed for a long time, naked, sharing his life with her, his thoughts, his memories. Later, he brought them a platter of food, and a bottle of wine. His evening patrols wouldn't begin for a little while longer, though he wasn't sure he'd be leaving her because of what happened the night before.

Samantha treasured this time as Ethan shared with her. He'd never exchanged histories with any woman before, that much he told her. A strange kind of magic surrounded the sharing, and the entire time, he kept his personal frequency open so that though their bodies had disconnected, even when he'd gone to the kitchen, she'd remained joined to him.

So, this was what it would be like, she thought, as she pushed a strand away from his face, tucking it behind his ear. Juice from a ripe peach he was eating, dripped down his chin. She leaned close and quickly caught it with her tongue and the moment seemed right again.

He pulled her on top of him and she rode him to the pinnacle, as once more he took from her vein.

When she lay in his arms, she laughed at the site of all the disturbed fruit and cheese and thought she could stay this way forever.

*** *** ***

Ethan held Samantha in his arms, his cock still inside her though only half-erect now. He'd come again and again. He was fired up because of her blood, and eased at the same time. His stomach no longer cramped; he was satisfied.

He didn't want to let her go, not now, not ever. He wished he understood the mystery of what was happening between them. The logical part of him kept calling him away from his house. By now, he would have been down at the training camp with his Guard, going over the terrain of Bergisson once more, devising new strategies, taking charge, ordering the patrols out, watching his men fly.

It was almost full-dark and still he didn't leave. He just held the woman, half-fae, half-human, tight in his arms, almost unable to release her. Definitely, unwilling.

He'd never experienced a connection like this before in his entire life, although shades of it felt very much like his birth family, the closeness he'd known with his sister and with his mother and father, now long gone.

Was that what Samantha had become to him in only a few short hours, his family?

That's what she felt like, something he must protect with everything in his body and soul, to his dying breath.

He loved…

Sweet Goddess, did he love her?

He lay with her quietly for a long time, even as he watched day give way completely to night.

Finally, his compulsion to be with his Guard, to protect Bergisson became a pulsing weight in his chest and he sighed heavily.

*** *** ***

"You need to contact Finn. I can feel it in you, like a boundless drive, stronger than any other part of you."

"Yep. Exactly. I'm sorry, Samantha."

She rose up and smiled down at him then kissed him once on the lips. "Never apologize for that. It's your finest quality, your loyalty and service. I value that about you. Remember that, Ethan."

He nodded.

She grabbed for a washcloth he'd provided and caught their shared wetness as she rolled off him, away from the platter of food. But she stayed in bed, letting him go about his business, taking the food away and putting it in the living area of his suite then heading into the shower.

The sight of him was beautiful and for that reason alone, to get to watch such masculine perfection walk around naked in a room she shared with him, was sufficient reason to stay.

She lay on her side enjoying the show as he showered, lathering up, his brow growing more furrowed by the second.

The connection of frequencies grew thinner and thinner until at last they dissolved, almost naturally, which was nice except now she didn't have the warmth of his spirit caressing her abdomen, because that was the only way she could explain what now felt cold and almost empty within her body.

She pressed a hand there, wondering if Ethan felt it as well.

I thought it for the best.

His voice in her mind startled her. *Were you reading my thoughts?*

No. But I was feeling the loss of your fae frequency and figured you might be experiencing something similar. Were you?

Yes. Such a strange emptiness.

He paused and she watched him turn into the spray so that the water hit the back of his neck. He parted his long hair and she had the best view.

I love what I'm looking at.

He shifted to look at her over his shoulder, to meet her gaze and for her benefit he smiled and flexed his butt-muscles a couple of times.

She laughed, her fingers now pressed to her lips. And for some reason, tears touched her eyes. How could she ever let a man like this go? But how could she stay?

*** *** ***

As Ethan toweled off, he tried not to think about how all he wanted to do was climb back in bed with Samantha and stay there for a decade just enjoying her.

But Finn tapped at his pathing frequency and he responded. *I'll be on my way in a few. Are we good out there?*

We've had a red-wind sighting at a community dance over at Caldwell. I'm sending two patrols over there now. I'm going with.

I'll join you.

You sure that's a good idea?

Ethan's gaze shifted to Samantha, whose eyes were closed. She looked so peaceful. *I have no idea anymore.*

Then sit tight and let me take a look. I'll be there in five minutes, then I'll report back.

Okay. Five minutes.

You got it.

Ethan ended the communication, then moved into his dressing area and put on his usual nightly battle-gear. When he opened his closet, he felt the need to thank his housekeeper, again, for how much she kept his gear in excellent shape. Several rows of leathers and woven shirts, even the a choice of long, sleeveless coats, ranged down the long metal rod. His leather boots gleamed with polish.

He tended to like extra metal on his leather pants and boots, medallions and what not. Gerrod had lifted a brow but Quinlan said he needed to be more wrecked in his choices; they were too mild for Grochaire's mastyr.

As he dressed, he heard Samantha hop in the shower and even start humming. His woman was content. He liked that. He'd done that for her. He understood that the sweet release of sex sent a lot of good things moving through the veins.

Using the hair dryer, he worked his hair to a state of half-dry knowing that a few minutes of flight would finish the job.

But he left the bathroom as soon as Samantha emerged from her shower. She was too damn appealing to be tolerated easily right now.

He waited for her but when she was dressed in jeans and a loose green blouse, tied at her hips, he thought that clothes or no clothes, he wanted her bad. He almost opened his arms, but he saw that she had a frown on her brow.

"What is it?"

"My faeness seems to be really alive right now, but I don't know why. I don't know what it means."

He went to her and took hold of her arm. "Just go with it, go with your instincts."

She looked up at him still frowning, her light blue eyes full of concern. "Would you go back to the conservatory with me? I think I should open up my fae-power with the crystal right now. I just sense something needs to be looked at."

"Then that's exactly what we'll do and don't worry about what's going on out there. I've been in contact with Finn."

"Okay. Let's do it."

He led her back to the conservatory, to the disk, and she walked straight beneath it. He moved in close behind her, his chest to her back. He slid his arms around her and he felt her engage her fae power and the latent igniting effect of the crystal as if by long habit. He knew she didn't understand how easily she'd taken to her faeness or even how powerful she really was.

The vibrations of her realm-energy passed through him like a warm wave of healing sensation. Whatever she felt, he was given a tremendous sense of peace, even of purpose, as he anchored her in the stream of light.

She leaned her head back against his chest, which caused him to breathe deeply as he thought yet again that he never wanted to let her go.

Ethan, I'm having a vision of the dance in Caldwell.

What do you see? His heart-rate increased, thumping heavily in his chest.

The Invictus, Finn, your guard.

Do you see Ry?

No, not yet, but Ethan, I don't think you're going to like this.

His heart might have stopped for a moment, then pressed on with dull thuds. *What?*

I'm there, I'm in this vision. I'm supposed to be there.

Without thinking, he stepped off the disk, pulling Samantha with him. Of course the resulting abrupt severing of power, caused her to list. Then she grabbed her head. "Oh, that hurts." She looked up at him. "Hey, don't ever do that again."

But his mind had only one-track. "I'll stay here with you or I'll leave a guard here with you, but you're not going anywhere the Invictus are, now or ever, do you hear me?"

He almost didn't believe that these words had come out of his mouth and Samantha couldn't have looked more surprised.

"This is no time to go Neanderthal on me. Save all that goodness for later."

Her words split his mind in two directions at once, the first taking him straight back to the bedroom, but the other reminded him of his most important purpose. "My job is to keep you alive."

She opened her mouth then closed it. Her gaze flitted over the room for a moment. He knew she was choosing her words carefully and then he felt it, a certain odd excitement emanating from her.

"Wait a minute. What else did you see? What's going on?"

"Ethan." She shook out her hands in the air. "Listen, I think . . . I mean, if what I saw can actually happen, I might have the power to break apart the Invictus pairs, and to save the enslaved realm-folk, those bonded to wraiths who were forced under duress to join them."

Ethan took both her arms in his hands. He shook his head back and forth. "But no one can do that. And you're not even fully realm, so how can you?"

"It's not *me*, Ethan. You're with me. It's *us*. *We* can do this thing. Together."

"Holy shit." He let go of her arms and moved in a quick circle. "What this would mean for our world. Oh, Samantha. And that's what you saw?" He faced her again and held her close.

"That's what I saw. So get me there and let's see what we can do."

Ethan had such confidence in her in this moment that he didn't hesitate to contact Finn and rearrange the patrols.

Once the plans were laid, he took her to the front door, then straight into the air, heading to Caldwell.

Chapter Nine

Samantha held tight to Ethan as he flew her in a northwesterly direction, higher in the air than she'd flown before because they'd be passing a tall, rolling set of hills and covering more country than she'd yet seen. Eight Guardsmen ranged on either side of them, their long coats flapping behind, a sound that gave Samantha some comfort.

Caldwell, an ancient place and built primarily of stone, was the largest town in the northwestern portion of Bergisson realm, and had a population of sixty thousand mixed realm residents. As high as they were, Samantha could see the central town square all lit up, but directly north of the city, a dozen Guardsmen battled the Invictus, at least twenty bonded pairs.

I'll be taking you to the square. Kyle's in charge of on-the-ground security right now. You'll be safe with him if I need to do battle.

He dropped into the square, landing at the far east edge, where the lights were dim and deserted of party-goers.

A handsome troll, with three beautiful forehead ridges hurried up to him. "Mastyr Ethan, we are so glad to see you and how well you look. Guardsman Finn has left several imprisoned wraith-pairs as you requested. We've never had a problem with the Invictus at one of our assemblies before."

His wife, an elven with strong features and her blond hair wrapped in a series of unique braids on top of her head, nodded. "They've never attacked this far north." Her troll husband slid his arm around her waist.

Samantha stepped off Ethan's boot as he said, "Mr. Mayor, I can see that you have your people well in hand."

Samantha glanced at the thinning crowd on the opposite side of the square.

The troll clucked his tongue. "There are always a few youths decrying the mistreatment of wraith-pairs and who made it almost impossible for the band to leave, but all that is settled. The square will be cleared in just a few more minutes." He shifted his gaze pointedly to Samantha.

Ethan introduced her and she offered her hand. The troll took it, smiling broadly. "And what a lovely fae resonance you have, my dear. Welcome to Caldwell and I hope at some time you'll be able to return and enjoy our fair town under better circumstances."

"I do as well." She took a moment to cast her gaze around the square. There were many small shops and most had potted evergreens out front, awnings, tables and chairs, even decorative lights.

She glanced at Ethan, willing him to understand that she wanted to be about their business.

He nodded to her. "Take us to the wraith-pairs, please."

The troll and the elf walked with great dignity toward the southeastern corner of the square, just opposite their current position. Samantha saw the Guardsman, Kyle, and several more standing in front of a municipal building.

Ethan leaned down to Samantha. "The police station is over there, where Kyle is waiting for us. He's probably holding the pairs inside."

As they reached the corner, near Kyle, she saw that the crowd, instead of continuing their departure had begun to return. She also heard many whisper, 'the mastyr is here' while others were saying, 'she must be the new blood rose'.

Samantha felt her cheeks grow warm. She'd always lived her life quietly and the most public she'd ever greeted was still just a smattering of one-on-one encounters when she would sell her jewelry during a street fair.

Ethan turned toward her, but his gaze scanned the square. He had one hand on her arm, very gently. "Where were you in the vision when we separated the bonded pairs?"

Glancing around the square, she saw that in the middle of a pedestrian-only track, lined by planters of flowers, benches, and an occasional well-lit street lamp, a central disk formed a cross-path. "There," she pointed. "The central circle."

"Of course," Ethan murmured.

As she moved in that direction, Ethan shouted orders to his Guard. "Bring all the wraith-pairs here. Now." His voice boomed above the murmuring crowds and the numerous flags flapping in the soft night breeze.

Finn suddenly called down from above. "Incoming friendlies, mastyr, but we have another pair here. The rest of the Invictus have retreated." He landed, sweaty from battle and placed his short-sword, in his scabbard attached to the leather cross-strap.

He offered Samantha a smile and a nod. "How you doin'?"

"Good. I'm good." And she was. For the first time since arriving in Bergisson she felt as though she had a purpose larger than just feeding a vampire.

The crowd began moving in. She almost said something to Ethan, but the mayor found a microphone and encouraged his people to remain well beyond the circle. The crowd shifted, moving away a few feet, which gave her some relief.

When the bonded pairs began arriving, the crowd booed heavily. Samantha remembered this from her vision as well, so she didn't try to stop it, nor did Ethan. For the destruction and the deaths the wraiths had caused, the least they deserved was a measure of public censure.

Ethan took her hand and held her gaze as he pathed, *How do you want to do this?*

I need to be standing in the center of the circle. I think it must be a fae-thing.

No doubt. He even smiled.

He led her there and she took her place, but her heart had set up a racket. Was she really going to do this, in front of God and everyone, something she still didn't understand?

But as Ethan gestured for the first pair to be brought to her, she knew what had to be done and her faeness rushed forward, removing her doubts. Something external must have shown as well, because the crowd almost as one, called out a big, surprised, 'Oh!'

What is it? She glanced up at Ethan.

He smiled at her. *You have an incredible aura right now, silver and violet. Beautiful.*

Samantha could only take his word for it.

As she turned her attention once more to the wraith pair who now stood five feet in front of them. She worked not to be revolted by the opaque skin of the wraith, the yellow fangs and dark lips, or even when the creature let out a shriek, which made the crowd jump. The wraith was bonded to a male troll, a muscular man with large dull eyes, not surprising since the bond robbed the bound individual of will and rational thought.

Samantha waved an arm in the wraith's direction, in a large arc, which, much to Samantha's surprise, released a flow of silver-violet energy. When that arc reached the wraith-pair, they fell together on their knees.

To Ethan, she pathed, *Put your arm around me and hold me steady. Something big is coming.*

I've got you.

She loved that he'd spoken just those words, but her fae power felt like a brutal force beneath her now and she trembled as she lifted her left arm aloft and brought it down in a quick, heavy strike between the shoulders of the pair.

Power released and not hers alone, but she felt Ethan's vampire power attach to her faeness and together the resulting energy forged an arc of light that split the bond in two.

The wraith fell sideways thrashing on the ground, but the troll stood there blinking several times.

A number of trolls moved in close. "Jonas? I think this is Jonas, from out at Evangeline Lake. He had a farm there a hundred years ago. Jonas, is that you?"

Ethan, have some of these realm-folk been bound for over a hundred years.

Yes, some longer.

My God.

The crowds murmurings grew louder and louder.

The troll looked around and took a step back as though astonished. "Where the hell am I?"

"It is Jonas. He always had a mouth on him, that one."

Some of the crowd laughed, but other trolls approached him and took him by the hand. Ethan called out. "Finn, take charge of him. We'll need to interrogate them all."

"Yes, mastyr."

Several more Guardsmen grabbed the wraith, but the creature didn't put up a fight, which surprised Samantha. "Is she physically hurt, demoralized, or what?" she asked quietly.

"They gain their power through the bond."

"That's horrible."

"It is. It's been a scourge for centuries. I'm hoping our new millennium will see the last of them."

"I do, too."

But the next bonded pair was hauled forward only this wraith fought long and hard against what he had seen happen to the first couple. He hissed and shrieked.

Ethan stood slightly in front of her, a protective position, as Samantha created the original arc of fae-power, shedding a silver-violet wave across the wraith's back. Once more the pair fell to their knees, this time the bonded mate was a tall fae woman who bore a lot of bruises on her arms.

With Ethan joining his power to hers once more, she repeated the process, and the bond was once more severed. The wraith fell forward prone and didn't move. He lay there twitching, his power completely gone.

Like the troll, however, the fae appeared stunned at first, her dull eyes eventually finding clarity as she began to focus on everything around her. Finally, she said, "Caldwell. This is Caldwell. And I'm free."

Her words brought a huge cheer rising from the residents. Huzzas followed, a long, triumphant string of them.

Samantha smiled as Ethan slid his arm around her waist and gave her a squeeze. She looked up at him. *We're doing some good here, aren't we?*

Yes, we are.

Samantha performed the service repeatedly until twelve wraith-pairs had been completely dissolved and the outlaw wraiths imprisoned. The recently liberated realm-folk were turned over to a team of fae who specialized in bondage crimes with a network of services that supported victims of all species.

As for Caldwell, since the Invictus force had not only been turned back well before the city's outskirts, and those wraith-pairs captured were now dissolved, it was party-time once more in the old stone square.

The mayor begged for Ethan and Samantha to participate in the festivities, but other than offering a few words at the microphone to wish everyone Goddess-speed, he excused himself for the sake of his Guard and his need to stay on patrol.

As the Guard took to the air, a deafening round of cheers and shouts followed.

Some even called out her name.

The sight of so many well-wishers in the stone-built town of Caldwell, added another layer to Samantha's confusion about just where she belonged.

*** *** ***

Ethan flew Samantha back to his primary residence. He'd come to love the feel of her next to him like this, her feet balanced on one foot as he drifted through the air.

Five Guardsmen accompanied them and Finn had the rest on patrols searching for more Invictus sign.

He might even have felt like he could let down a little, but something restless moved through his ranks, like they each caught a distant jarring vibration that kept his troops on edge.

I need to be with my troops.

Now? Tonight?

Yes. Something's going on.

But I thought…

What did you think? Because we'd worked together?

Yes, because we'd saved a number of your people, bringing them out of years, even decades of captivity, that you might be able to stop, to take a little time with me. This wasn't easy you know.

She'd grown stiff in his arms.

Now this felt familiar, the few times he'd allowed a woman to get too close; she wanted more from him than he could give.

He needed to set her straight, so he pathed, *Bergisson comes first, it always will.*

I get that, or thought I did. But Finn can take charge now and then. He's more than capable.

The fact that Finn had been telling him something similar for the past decade didn't ease his mind or his temper. He shot back, *And now you're an expert on battling the Invictus?*

Not exactly. But I am an expert when a man is being a dick, which you are right now, by the way.

He almost smiled, but he was too edgy to be that amused and why did he have to like it when she called him a dick?

Whether or not you're right about this, I have to go out.

Do you want to at least check to see if there's another vision you can use? Seems to me I did some good just now.

He wasn't sure why he was being so pricklish, but he relented a little. *Yes, you did a lot of good and I'm proud of you. But, Samantha, whatever the future holds, Bergisson comes first. I have a million realm-souls on my shoulders and I feel them every living day of the year.*

I know you do.

He didn't like that she fell suddenly quiet, then he knew why. He felt her doubts like a wave washing over him, tightening his gut a little more, making his edginess reach that jumping off point.

And it ticked him off that even after all she'd just experienced and accomplished in Caldwell, that she would think for even a second that she didn't belong here.

You're thinking about Shreveport.

And my grandmother's home.

Shit. His personal frequency tightened up into a knot. He couldn't bear the thought that she might choose to return to Shreveport. But why couldn't she see the value of staying, even staying with him?

Then he'd hardly made it easy for her. If anything, his realm had been one long nightmare, including his own Neanderthal conduct that got sprung at the slightest hint of another male getting close to her.

Still, it irritated him that she didn't see that she belonged here. But then maybe she was more like Andrea than he wanted to admit.

When he touched down outside his primary residence, he'd never been more grateful than to see Vojalie and Davido. They sat in chairs near the fireplace, the baby monitor between them, Bernice probably tucked away in her crib.

Their presence gave him something else to focus on besides his desire to haul Samantha to his bedroom and either give her a good talking to about how she need to shape up and make a decision to stay, or to throw her on the back and prove who she belonged to once and for all.

Instead, he let her precede him while he remained near the front door hoping for his temper to cool. At the same time, he felt that same vibration in the air, that something wasn't right, that something big was going on.

Vojalie gave him one long look then focused all her attention on Samantha as the latter shared the events of the evening.

Ethan turned away from her and contacted Finn. *How does it look out there?*

Something's on the wind. Hell, I thought with the Invictus retreating at Caldwell, we'd be settling down for the night. Instead, I don't know.

I felt it, too, all the way back to my house, which is where I am, by the way.

And you'd rather be here.

In the air, yes, patrolling. I'm about ready to crawl out of my skin.

Samantha okay?

Yeah, she's fine. Chatting with Vojalie.

Well, that's good. She's safe. Odd that Ry didn't show up.

Yeah, I thought he would.

Hold on. One of my men is signaling me. I'm out near Sweet Gorge. Looks like we've got Invictus sign, just a small party.

Check in later.

Will do.

When the conversation ended, Ethan rubbed the back of his neck. Damn, but didn't he hate this, standing around like a fool, waiting for a bomb to drop.

Samantha, who had sat down on a couch opposite Vojalie glanced up at him. "What's wrong?"

He paced now and couldn't seem to stop himself. "I don't know. Invictus out at Sweet Gorge, for one thing."

"You want to go out there, don't you?"

He stopped and faced her. "I do. Finn's there now."

"Then you should go."

Vojalie said, "But shouldn't you maybe use Samantha's faeness and check for a vision?"

Samantha's brow rose and she held her hands apart as she met his gaze, then her gaze grew cloudy and she rose from her chair. "I see something."

He moved toward her, hurrying down the stairs. "Okay tell me." .

When he caught her hands, her eyesight seemed to clear and she said, "I saw a number of dead out there, at Sweet Gorge."

"Was I there?"

"You were looking down at them."

"And you?"

She shook her head. "No, I wasn't there."

"I've got to go."

"Go." She even gave him a little shove.

"I'll leave five Guardsmen here to watch over the house."

She nodded.

He hurried back to the door and closed it behind him. He left instructions for his Guardsmen to stay on alert and patrol only the immediate vicinity and to let no one in, then he flew hard in an easterly direction toward the place his family had died forty years ago.

*** *** ***

Samantha felt that something was wrong, but she couldn't put her finger on it. For one thing, she'd never quite seen Ethan like this before, as though every nerve in his body had been lit on fire. He always had an edge, but this was something more.

She turned to Vojalie who sat forward in her chair watching her closely. "What is it?"

Samantha shook her head. "I don't know what's going on, but I don't like the state he's in. It didn't seem natural to him. Did it to you?"

"Ethan was always quick to move."

But Samantha had been with him very intimately for the past several days and she'd tapped his personal frequency. This wasn't just his usual energy, his drive toward his care of Bergisson. No, something was wrong.

Her mind slid over all the events that had happened, about Ethan and their connection, the recent salvation of wraith-bonded realm-folk, and earlier in the conservatory when Ry had almost had her.

What was it she'd felt then, that dark fae force?

Images rushed through her mind again, of the massacre at Sweet Gorge. She could see it all now, as Ethan must have seen it so long ago.

She willed herself to grow very still. She blocked the images, setting them aside. She needed to understand something very clearly right now and it had to do with her mother and what happened the night Ethan's family was killed.

She turned to Vojalie. "I'll be in the conservatory reading my mother's journals."

"At least take one of the Guardsmen with you."

"Good idea."

Once Samantha had a vampire in tow, she returned to the bedroom she'd been given when she first arrived at Ethan's house. She sorted through her mother's journals and chose the last one written about Bergisson, before she left for good.

Taking it to the conservatory where the Guardsman patrolled the edges of the vast, plant-filled space, she sat down on the bench nearest her door and scanned the last several entries.

Andrea had experienced confusion. Horrific images had rolled relentlessly through her mind, day and night, past visions that had transformed into real events, disasters imprinted forever on her memory.

And Samantha could relate except for one thing: Andrea never spoke of an ancient fae entity interfering with her, or muddling her mind. She did however say more than once that she didn't know how much more she could take.

The final entry was now familiar to Samantha, because Andrea had been inundated with images of a terrible massacre at Sweet Gorge, images that Andrea had been sure had occurred a hundred years prior. More confusion, dizziness.

But Andrea had laid the state of her mind down to grief, the images she believed belonged to the past, her confusion of mind. So, she'd made her decision. She'd needed a change. She'd needed to leave Bergisson.

Samantha stood up, the journal falling from her lap to the pavers at her feet.

She got it. She finally understood exactly what had happened to her mother. The fae of unknown but ancient and dark origin had been afflicting her for months, but Andrea hadn't understood what had been going on, what had been happening to her.

She reached her hand toward the Guardsman, but only then did she realize that once more the conservatory was full of strange waves and movement. The Guardsman lay prone on the floor, still breathing, but clearly unconscious.

She smelled the ancient fae now, a terrible stench like something that had rotted at the bottom of a garbage bin.

Then Ry appeared, holding out his hand to her. "Come, Samantha. It's time to fulfill the best part of my plans for you. We're going to Sweet Gorge and finish what should have ended there forty years ago. You and I can do this together because my fae friend will help us. She's promised untold riches and power once we bond. But come. Let me fly you to Ethan so you can say good-bye."

Samantha took in his words, but her mind already felt full of black smoke, so she didn't quite get what he was trying to say.

But she heard Ethan's name and she wanted to be with him. Ry could take her to Ethan.

She stumbled more than once as she made her way to Ry, who stood on the central disk. When she saw the glitter in his eye, she knew it would be a mistake to go with him, but how could she refuse him? She could feel his need.

Once she reached him, the crystal apex lit up her fae power and strengthened her, which in turn apparently gave Ry a rush because he cried out, "Sweet Goddess, I could live in this stream of energy forever."

A female voice intruded, very softly. "Ry, take your prize to Sweet Gorge and complete the bond. Do it now."

"Yes, Mistress."

Leaving the house proved a simple thing since Vojalie and Davido had retired to their rooms.

Ry took her in his arms, flew her to the front door, and straight up into the air past Ethan's Guardsmen.

Samantha wasn't surprised that the powerful vampires hadn't seen her. The ancient fae clearly had many tricks, but what would she find at Sweet Gorge?

*** *** ***

With Finn nearby, and fifty of his Guard spread along the southern ridge, Ethan stared down into the gorge.

He'd been right. Something big was on the wind, a fulfillment of the vision Samantha had seen, the one that Quinlan would soon take part in.

One of his Guardsmen had already been killed and lay deep in the gorge while two others were trapped in some sort of strange webbing that neither he, nor any of his men could explain.

He paced near Finn. The rest of his entire Bergisson force was on the way, coming from every part of his realm.

Even Quinlan had sent for two hundred of his Guard from Grochaire and was waiting for them to arrive at the far eastern realm-to-realm access point in order to bring them over to Sweet Gorge.

He shoved his hands through his hair, while images of what the gorge had looked like forty years ago kept flashing through his brain, unbidden, as though placed there to torture him.

He grew edgier by the second. He needed to act, but Finn kept warning him to wait.

Another roll of images as the past rose up to torment him: Bodies everywhere, beyond the web holding the two warriors. Sweet Goddess, he could see women and children bloodied, drained, dead. Men as well. Realm-folk of all kind. A woman held her troll-babe in her arms, both dead.

He shouted into the air.

A hand clapped him hard on the shoulder. "Ethan!" Finn called sharply.

Ethan whirled, his mind encased with too much gore and his heart weighed down with guilt and pain. "They died here."

"Who died here? Your family, you mean? Fuck, Ethan. What's going on?"

"I have to help them."

"Help, who?"

"My mother and father."

Finn grabbed both his shoulders in his hands. "Look at me!"

Ethan stared hard at Finn. He focused harder. Finally, the images left and he pressed fingers against his eyes. "Sweet Goddess, I'm being tormented by the past."

"Don't think about it."

He shook his head. He felt better. "Where's Quinlan?"

"ETA 10 minutes. His Guard just reached the access point. He told us to hang tough."

Ethan nodded. Movement from the web below drew his attention. One of his men struggled to escape, but the web tightened and he called out in anguish as the tendrils cut him.

Ethan made his decision. "At least I can do this. I can get them the hell out of there."

He launched with Finn calling out. "No. It's a trap. Ethan!"

He stopped before he reached the web. He knew enough not to touch the webbing, but that's when a second layer released and the next thing he knew he was spun midair then pinned on his back, held in place by a top web.

He couldn't move. Even the smallest shift of his body, sent tendrils up from the netting hooking him in tighter.

He'd never felt so helpless, which pissed him off. He balled his hands into fists, but now his hands were covered with tendrils that pulled and clawed at him, breaking skin and causing him to bleed.

He had to lie still, maybe the hardest thing in the world for him, to just stop. And do nothing.

Worse followed as he stared up at the ridge, where Finn stood with at least fifty of his Guardsmen because suddenly Ry appeared. But he wasn't alone; he held Samantha in his arms. And if that wasn't strange enough, somehow he was cloaked from view.

A stench reached him, of filth and decayed matter, a thick odor laced with fae magic.

Then he understood: *enthrallment. Fae enthrallment power, like nothing he'd ever known before.*

She was here. The dark fae entity, the cause of all the trouble at the gorge. He understood several things at once, that she'd somehow gotten past all five of his Guards and that she was using Ry and intended to use Samantha to take control of Bergisson.

He watched Finn weave on his feet, then cover his face with his hands. The same thing happened to his entire Guard up and down the ridge.

Ry pierced Ethan's mind telepathically. *It won't be long now and I'll take back what is mine.*

Ethan tried to respond, to yell at Ry, to talk sense to him, but Ry cut the communication quickly.

He also attempted to reach Samantha, but he couldn't path to her, couldn't access her telepathy.

At the same time, images of the massacre returned and once more slammed through his mind. He knew he was being messed with, which helped him to understand at last what must have happened to Andrea, that the ancient fae had tormented her as well. Because what else could have prompted such a faithful woman to leave her home forever?

Ethan went very still inside and the images of forty years ago melted away, as though his own turmoil and bitterness had kept them there.

He was left with the difficult reality that he could have been wrong all this time about Samantha's mother and what had really happened at Sweet Gorge that night. Until recently, he'd thought it had simply been a large, random Invictus attack that Andrea had seen in a dream but refused to report. She'd deserted Bergisson that night, leaving him to clean up the worst disaster his realm had ever experienced.

Guilt had covered him for decades, the sure knowledge that if he'd been more responsible, his family wouldn't have died.

Now, tonight, in this moment, the truth rose to hit him harder still that Ry, along with a powerful enemy just barely making itself known to the Nine Realms, had planned and executed the massacre that night. Davido had been right after all: The sheer numbers would have overpowered him and he would have died as well.

Why forty years had elapsed before a second attempt, he didn't know, but he had a strong sense that this day had been developing for decades, waiting for the arrival of Samantha to give Ry sufficient power to take the prize he sought, with the help of course of the dark fae force.

Samantha.

His thoughts turned to her, as Ry once more smiled down at him, holding her close. What he waited for, Ethan didn't know, but he felt sure some timing was at work, maybe an Invictus force that needed to be moved into place.

But Samantha, Andrea's very own daughter, had been the biggest surprise of all. He'd spent barely three nights with her, yet somehow his life had been transformed completely into something he hadn't even realized until this moment. At long last love had pierced the hard shell of his guilt and opened up a hope that he could have a better life, one in which a woman slept in his bed, listened to his thoughts as he listened to hers, worked through difficult issues, and in the end became something *more* together than each would have been separately.

How changed Samantha was as well, though maybe she didn't see realize it. But from the first, he'd caught a glimpse of her solitary life, not much different from his, though each enjoyed their labors. She'd been alone and now she had a new heritage, new gifts, even a new family if she could embrace it.

He didn't want this to be the end, for Samantha to be bound and enslaved to Ry for what would amount to centuries and he didn't want to die, but here he was caught in a kind of netting that cut at him if he so much as half-flexed his pinkie-muscle.

New images rushed through his mind, of meeting Samantha for the first time, of making love to her in his bed and feeding from her vein -- Sweet Goddess, all the times he'd fed from her! -- then of anchoring her while she gathered strength from the crystals whether at the fae Guildhall or within his conservatory. He recalled how he'd experienced such a pure, healing energy flow through him as she accessed her faeness in a beautiful stream of violet-silver light. And she'd healed him of five decades of blood-starvation, of a curse he'd accepted when his mastyr-power had arrived all those years ago. Suffering, pain, and the weight of realm-responsibility had all been eased by Samantha.

Now Ry had her.

She'd slipped through Ethan's grasp like water pouring through his fingers.

And as his ranks struggled beneath the mind-control of the dark fae presence.

But to add to the present horrors, suddenly Invictus wraith-pairs moved in from behind, hundreds of them, surrounding his men.

And Ethan couldn't lift a finger to do anything about it.

He tried to reach either Finn or Samantha telepathically, but somehow Ry blocked these communications.

There seemed to be no way out.

And Ry threw his head back and laughed, a hateful victorious sound that forged a fire of revenge in Ethan's veins.

*** *** ***

Samantha knew Ry would begin the bonding process soon and that he would do whatever it took to bind her to him right now, on the ridge of Sweet Gorge, with Ethan trapped below beside two of his men in some kind of strange netting. The stench of the dark fae presence reeked now, all along the ridge and down into the gorge.

She was here, that which had the power right now to end Samantha's freedom forever, to take Ethan's life, to destroy the Bergisson Guard and to control Ry and therefore the future of the realm, maybe even of all Nine Realms.

How foolish she'd been to think that only her choice between Shreveport and Bergisson was at stake, when right now her freedom for what would become centuries would soon be lost as well as Ethan's life.

Ry had wanted him dead for a long, long time. She could smell that stench on him as well, that he intended Ethan's death, hopefully executing both her bondage and Ethan's demise at the same time.

He'd drink from her while he bound her and because the fae entity still muddled Samantha's mind, it seemed an impossible situation to her, that there was no way out. She would succumb to Ry, he would grow in sufficient power, and he'd slay Ethan.

Ethan.

A calmness came over her when she thought about him, all that they'd been through. Unless something miraculous happened, the life as she'd known it and the extraordinary experiences she'd shared with Ethan would end in the next few minutes.

Despair ran through her as a deep awareness rose that what had arrived in Club Prave in Shreveport wasn't just a mastyr vampire looking to uphold the law of his realm, but a man she could love. How surprising, sudden, unexpected and unbelievable, but yes, love had come to her in the form of a vampire.

Yes, she was part-realm, that much was true, but somehow her heritage didn't factor in at all. She loved Ethan, that he made her laugh, that he made love to her like a god, that he was kind and considerate, that he loved Bergisson, something Ry would never understand and never be able to do.

Ry wanted power and he wanted to rule, as a dictator would, with full control.

Ethan wanted his realm-folk safe. That was all. He wanted his people safe to make their livings, to fall in love, to create families and to build future generations for centuries to come.

Ry didn't care if he brought all Nine Realms down to nothing, just so long as he was Mastyr of Bergisson.

In that moment, she made her decision, the one that had seemed so impossible a few hours ago, whether to remain in Bergisson or not, whether to take up a life as Ethan's blood rose, or not, whether to engage with the powerful fae community or not.

She wanted to stay, in part because she now understood that the dark fae presence had ruined her mother's life, had so troubled her mind, forcing images through her, that she'd been unable to cope with the visions, the blood and gore, the pain and anguish, so she had left her world behind and made a new life in Shreveport.

Now Samantha had come home, to take up what was rightfully hers if she wanted it.

And yet what stood in her way right now seemed unconquerable: A vampire without a conscience who had complete physical power over her.

But was there a way out, a way to possibly connect with Ethan?

After all they'd been through, surely, she could establish a connection and break the control that the dark fae entity had over Sweet Gorge.

But how?

One thing she did understand, the calmer she remained, the less muddled her mind was. If she struggled or tried to break free, it was as though these actions alone brought the dark force once more invading her mind and removing her ability to reason.

She therefore took deep breaths and waited.

She wouldn't be able to do this alone. As calmly as she could, she opened her telepathic frequency to Ethan, but Ry entered her mind. *Can't let you do that, sweetheart. You're mine now.*

She said nothing in response.

She waited.

A female voice intruded. "Now is the time, Ry. Take your prize and Bergisson will be yours."

Ry pushed her hair away from her throat. *I'm going to make you mine, Samantha, right here on the ridge, in front of Ethan, the Goddess, and everyone else.*

Unwilling to give him the satisfaction of her fear or to alert the fae entity to her clear mind, she remained very still, but every ounce of her spirit became focused solely on Ethan.

No more holding back with him.

Whatever he needed from her right now, was his for the taking. She met and held his gaze, hoping he could somehow intuit her intentions, her love, her willingness to do anything that was needed in this situation.

She mouthed the words, 'For Bergisson'.

His brows lifted slightly, then a slight curve touched his lips.

Chapter Ten

Ethan's heart swelled, a physical movement that the webbing couldn't touch.

He loved Samantha, with all his heart. He knew that now, deep in his spirit, in the combined frequencies that made up his vampire nature. If he'd had any doubt before about her worth, or whether he should give himself to her fully, she had just washed them away as she mouthed 'for Bergisson'.

She got him, she got his world, and she got her purpose in his realm and what he felt was joy, pure and simple.

He felt her calmness as well, a mirror of his own, that their current circumstances, each bound so heavily and unable to move, had quieted their respective thoughts and movements, given each time to think and to reassess.

Mostly, he knew she was with him, all the way.

Hope began a powerful journey back through his veins, rebuilding his determination to somehow find a way out of this deadly situation, but with new insights, primarily that he wasn't alone in his command.

He shifted his gaze back to Ry, now holding Samantha closer.

Ry pathed Ethan again. *This is for you, Ethan, for taking what belonged to me. So now I'm taking what you desire and returning Bergisson to her rightful owner at the same time.*

But Ethan didn't respond. He remained very still, turning his attention solely to Samantha.

Ry drew his lips back, letting his fangs emerge fully, two wet, powerful points.

Ethan watched the fangs strike. His body reacted on instinct, a sharp jerk which much to his surprise caused the web, just for a split-second, to give way.

Startled, he looked around. Why hadn't the web tightened instead? Cut him up?

What had changed?

Only one thing: Ry had pierced Samantha's neck, which must have meant that once he shifted his attention to her, it broke a connection elsewhere.

His first instinct was to break free, right now, and do battle with Ry. But his impulses had put him here in the web in the first place, so he remained still.

Again, what had changed?

Then, exactly how much had changed?

He ignored his rage at watching Ry drink from Samantha though even at that distance, he felt Ry's personal frequency pounding against her faeness, demanding entrance and submission. If Ry wore her down and bound her to him, she'd be lost forever.

So would Bergisson because Ry would have the power he'd been seeking, in tandem with the ancient fae force, to do whatever he liked.

Except something wasn't right, wasn't working, and the shift had occurred the moment Ry began to feed. He suspected it meant that the ancient fae force had to work with a minion in order to hold her power over so many realm at once. And Ry was her minion, in servitude to her, and the vessel she used to carry out her expansive enthrallment.

But if he could move in the web, then what else could he do right now, while Ry's attention was focused on Samantha?

He glanced at the Invictus and another question rose: With his entire Guard enthralled, why hadn't the Invictus attacked them, unless they couldn't. And that was the other part of the answer, that the enthrallment was universal and had encompassed the Invictus as much as his Guard.

There were limits, therefore, to the ancient fae's power and apparently, in order to function at top levels, she needed her minion's full attention.

She didn't have that now, not with Ry lost in the sublime taste of Samantha's blood, which meant he had a handful of minutes to organize a counter offensive. The fae's enthrallment still operated, just not at full force.

He shifted his attention to Finn and attempted telepathy. *Finn?*

His second-in-command lifted his chin slowly and met his gaze. *You feel it, as well, the release of the thrall, at least to a degree?*

Enough for us to talk and to strategize. I know I could leave this web right now, for instance, but that would alert Ry and he's the key. The fae force that has control of Sweet Gorge right now, must have his focus to do what she does.

I alerted the Guard to remain still until further ordered.

Good move. Smart.

I also got through to Quinlan. He arrives in three minutes. Where do you want him when he comes in? He's got part of his Grochaire Guard with him.

Let me contact Samantha. Hold steady and keep pretending that you're enthralled. Tell everyone.

Ethan shifted his focus back to his blood rose, ignoring his ever-present need to tear Ry apart. He remained calm and approached her mind. *Samantha, can you receive this?*

Yes. Thank God. Ethan, ever since he started drinking a lot of my confusion has lessened, but I wasn't sure what to do, whether contacting you would alert him, but everything has changed, hasn't it?

Yes, for the moment, so long as he feeds from you.

Which means we have a shot. Ethan, just tell me what to do.

Can you access your fae vision again? Can you see the future?

Absolutely.

He took a moment to test the binding tendrils and when he moved his left hand the webbing gave way. He could still free himself if he wanted.

He closed his eyes forcing himself to hold back. How many times had he screwed up in the past because he was in such a hurry to take charge, not to let others lead?

So, he calmed himself once more and waited for Samantha, focusing on her.

He felt her settle into herself more deeply and after a moment she pathed, *On the other side of the gorge is a stretch of land that the ancient fae has kept hidden from view. I see barracks, maybe a training camp. But there are two hundred wraith-pairs ready to do battle, ready to slaughter your guard. Now I see Quinlan and his men attacking that group.*

Ethan murmured, *Good, that's good. Now what about the gorge itself, me, my Guard?*

She tells him the rest of what she's seen in the vision and he's dumbfounded but he'll also have to trust her and he'll have to leave most of the fighting to others.

Can you do this, Ethan? You'll have to leave the battling to everyone else? Can you do that?

That's when he understood the full breadth of what Samantha's presence in his life had come to mean, that now he could do what had before been impossible. *Yes, I can turn the battle over to Finn and Quinlan: I trust each with my life.*

Good. But she sounded strained, her voice faint in his mind. *Because the time has almost come. I'm very weak right now and his personal frequency is pounding hard, demanding admittance.*

Samantha, just tell me, what is the signal for our forces to begin battling?

When I fall to the ground.

Oh, sweet Goddess. He didn't know if he could bear the sight without reacting before he should.

You can do this, Ethan. Now, let everyone else know. It won't be long. Maybe half-a-minute from now.

Ethan closed down the communication and sought Finn and Quinlan. He outlined what Samantha had related to him. Each was ready. Quinlan had brought a hundred-and-twenty-five of his Guard from Grochaire. This might just work.

He could only watch now and wait for the signal.

But nothing happened. Instead, Ry kept drinking like he couldn't stop.

Ethan pathed to Samantha. *He won't stop. Samantha, we have to do something together to break him right now.*

So weak.

I'm going to send my personal frequency straight at you. Just turn and embrace me with your faeness, that'll give you some strength. Once that happens, I'll hit Ry with a jolt of my own. My guess is, his rage will fly off the charts and instead of reconnecting with the ancient fae, he'll want to battle me. When he breaks free of you and turns in my direction, just drop to the ground as planned.

Okay.

Using all the power he could muster, he focused on his personal frequency and sent it straight at Samantha. She responded and the moment her faeness touched him, he sent a stream of power through the pathway, found Ry's frequency and sent a jolt straight toward him.

As predicted, Ry came off Samantha's neck roaring his rage and turning at the same time toward Ethan, his eyes blood red.

Samantha dropped to the ground.

And all hell broke loose.

Finn and Kyle attacked Ry with short-swords so that he had to shift his attention away from Ethan, away from the dark fae, and toward to fellow Guardsmen holding nothing back.

At the same time, Ethan's Guard turned on the Invictus and the battle was on, more visceral than usual since they didn't have time to form the battle shield. The sound of metal weapons clashed in the night air.

Ethan used his dagger to release himself from the now powerless web-trap, doing the same for the Guardsmen next to him. He ordered both to engage in battle.

He heard a wailing sound and the stench of the ancient fae grew strong around him. She'd lost control. He tried to see her, to find her, but she had tremendous shielding capacity.

But apparently without Ry, she was incapable of action.

Ethan shot up the gorge, but instead of engaging in the fight, he picked Samantha up in his arms, and carried her away from the fighting.

She was very weak, but she pathed, *Fly me to the monolith. I've felt the crystals calling to me for the past few minutes. I can find strength there.*

He took her to the eastern ridge and the rock outcropping that had once held the waterfall. He carried her to the ledge from which the water had once spilled and fed Sweet Gorge Stream.

But the ancient fae magic clung to the space and at the same time her stench grew stronger.

The fae is here.

He nodded. *Just ignore her. She can't act apart from Ry, not in this form.*

I can sense that as well.

She breathed deeply and smiled. He felt her strength return just as her blood-supply began renewing at light-speed.

Ethan looked at the cave-like opening from which the water had at one time emerged. "Samantha, did you see this in your vision?"

She shook her head, staring into the cave.

"But you can feel the crystals?"

"Yes, absolutely." She stood straighter now, stronger.

Ethan turned her to face him. "What do you think would happen if you engaged these crystals right now, with me, with our joint power?"

Her lips parted. "Do you think we could break this apart? Remove the dam?"

"Maybe. Maybe that's what we're meant to do, but there's something I need to say first."

"What?" She looked startled.

"I love you. Just wanted to say it. But I love you, Samantha."

Tears filled her eyes. "I love you, too." She threw herself into his arms and he held her tight.

He wanted to prolong the moment, but they had a job to do first.

He nodded in three quick dips of his chin. "Good. We can talk later."

She smiled, she even chuckled. Then she leaned her head against his chest, and he felt her open her faeness to the wealth of blue crystals inside the upper birth of the monolith that flattened to a long plain to the east, a place partially hidden all these years.

He felt the flow of her power begin and saw that the air surrounding her now filled with violet-silver light.

But nothing happened.

She looked up at him, a question in her eyes. Then she drew back.

"We need to be bonded," he said. "Is that what you're sensing? In order for this to happen?"

"Yes." She smiled. "I'm ready, but I'll only do this if you are as well."

Peace flowed through him like nothing he'd ever known before. "I want to bond with you more than I've wanted anything in my long-lived life. Will you have me, Samantha, as deeply flawed as I am, impulsive and stubborn, will you have me?"

"I will. But will you have me? I've not been the easiest person to be around over the last few days and I'm stubborn, too."

He stared into light blue eyes and knew he'd never forget this moment, of love passing back and forth between them, the sweetest vibration he'd ever known. "Without question."

"I love you, Ethan with all my heart."

He nodded and pulled her into his arms. He let her feel his answering love as he opened his personal frequency to her. At the same time, her faeness became a vast world for him to explore as she held nothing back. His frequency passed inside and she embraced him fully.

I willingly bind myself to you, Mastyr Ethan of Bergisson.

And I with you, Samantha of Shreveport and now my realm.

The bond clicked in place, and sent a responding vibration back through his frequency and up and out. The same happened for Samantha as she drew back and arched her neck.

Their combined energy flowed around them expanded more and more.

Suddenly the ancient fae cried out a long, shrill, 'no', a plaintive cry that faded as did her smell.

At the same time, he heard rumblings from deep in the earth.

I have to path you into the air. Things are about to explode.

Do it!

Ethan whipped her off the ledge and up into the night air. He kept rising, which was a damn good thing because a wall of blue crystals suddenly shot out of the opening, a beautiful spray that would have cut both of them to ribbons. Following close behind the crystal, a rush of water plummeted down the steep stone face of the ridge, falling sixty feet to the bottom of the gorge below.

And Sweet Gorge Stream was reborn.

Ethan kept rising, however, holding Samantha close, turning in a slow half-circle. His forces along the south ridge had overcome the Invictus during that time, while Kyle and Finn, fighting shoulder-to-shoulder, forced Ry down the side of the gorge, half-levitating as each struck, half-stumbling on the earth.

Ry might have gained more power from Samantha's blood, and as a mastyr he was more powerful generally, but Finn and Kyle were both powerful Guardsmen and together they were able to keep pushing him back until he finally took off flying west, as water began pouring down the stream.

Ethan needed to go after him, but not until Samantha was safe.

"I see Quinlan," she called out. "There, flying above the east ridge, just like in the vision. He has his Guard with him."

He pivoted and sure enough, Quinlan flew, his dark eyes on fire, his fangs half-emerged, a sure sign he'd been in battle. He held his short-sword aloft and let out a battle cry.

When he reached Ethan, he levitated next to him, a breeze whipping his long black hair in strands over his face. "We've got them, all of them. There were two-hundred pairs but we subdued them and saved as many as we could." He glanced at Samantha. "I'm hoping you'll be able to rescue more of our enslaved realm-folk."

"Of course."

Ethan felt different, changed. He'd crossed a final bridge and he wouldn't go back. He'd bonded with Samantha and maybe for that reason alone he was able to address Quinlan, another mastyr vampire, as he said, "Would you look after her? I can't let Ry get away this time."

"Absolutely."

While in midair, he passed over her, and though a quiver of possessiveness swept through him at the sight of Samantha's arm around Quinlan's neck, he ignored the sensation and whipped around to fly, as he had never flown before, west, after Ry. He couldn't let Ry reconnect with the ancient fae again.

But because of the new bond with Samantha, he had speed now, greater than before. He flew faster and faster and soon found Ry flying over La Fourche Lake.

A few seconds more, he grabbed for Ry, catching his shoulder strap and giving a sharp tug, which sent him into a downward spin toward the water.

But Ry caught himself and when he flew upward toward Ethan, he had his short-sword in his left hand and in his right he gathered power.

Ethan felt the power he'd gained by joining with Samantha at the waterfall monolith and it was a killing power. But he didn't hesitate. Instead, he let it fly as he raced in Ry's direction.

Because Ry had released his energy as well, sparks flew, but much closer to Ry, which parted his lips and put a scowl on his face. He might even have cursed.

He turned and headed down, toward the water, then leveled out along the surface, but the nearby hamlet of La Fourche was too close. Ry could get lost in the narrow stone streets, hide out, take hostages.

Ethan couldn't let that happen.

He geared up for another energy stream, flicked his wrist and caught Ry in his back, sending him headfirst into the water, skipping like a stone three times because of his speed.

Ethan flew slower as he neared Ry, now face down. With that much speed he could have broken his neck.

He got close enough to reach for Ry's arm, then he saw the air bubbles, and withdrew just in time. Ry whipped around, his short-sword moving in a swift arc. He would have taken off Ethan's arm.

At the same time, Ethan used his sword and caught Ry under his collar bone and up through his neck.

He looked surprised as Ethan withdrew the blade. Blood flowed as he slid back into the water.

Ethan reached in and grabbed the back of the coat, hauling him in a quick levitated flight to shore, dropping him on the grass. Blood flowed and bubbled as he gasped his last breaths. Ethan knew he was trying to self-heal, but he'd delivered a mortal wound.

"All this time," Ethan said, dropping to sit on the grass a few feet away. "All this time, you served in the Guard yet you were planning these attacks."

Ry could barely speak, but he said between gasps for air. "I hated you. I always did. Fucking usurper." His body went lax and his eyes dilated fully.

Ry was dead.

Ethan stared out at the lake, now settling down from the waves Ry's body had created. Ducks swam in and out of reeds at the far side. Realm-folk had begun to gather at the village end.

He breathed deeply, grateful that it was over.

He pathed to Finn, asking for an update.

All the Invictus pairs are subdued. We're rounding them up on the east plain. It's lined with barracks. Ry must have used it as a training camp. How did we not know?

Dark fae enthrallment and shielding. He probably had a lot of help. This isn't a simple thing that's going on.

No. It isn't.

Ethan then called for Guardsmen to take care of Ry's body.

As soon as they arrived, he returned to Samantha.

Fortunately, Quinlan had deposited her on the south ridge and had returned to his Guard. He was gearing up to get his men back to Grochaire Realm.

Finn had summoned the fae healers, who were at work, moving among the injured. Even Vojalie had arrived and now stood next to Samantha an arm around her shoulders. Other workers carted off the dead to the morgue.

Ethan flew slowly over Sweet Gorge. The dry wasteland would soon be renewed. Maybe the time had come to build a memorial for those who had perished in the massacre.

He'd see to it himself.

But something vibrated within his chest, and instinctively he glanced toward Samantha. He felt her, in a new way now that they were bonded, and he could tell that she needed him.

*** *** ***

Samantha watched Ethan turn and head in her direction. He'd been looking down at Sweet Gorge and she'd felt a variety of sensations move through him from terrible sadness, to hope, then reverence.

He looked magnificent, even though he was blood-spattered and sweaty, his long gorgeous hair in tangles, but he glowed with the look of a man who'd triumphed and who now knew some peace.

She didn't need to ask if Ry was gone; she could feel it in Ethan as clearly as she knew he felt overwhelmed by all that had happened, the same way she felt.

Even with Vojalie next to her, she needed Ethan right now. She'd begun to tremble from the exertion and stress. He slid his arm around her and she leaned against him closing her eyes and holding him hard.

Quinlan flew close but didn't land. "I have to get my men back to Grochaire. Looks like I've got signs of Invictus in three different sectors."

"Need help?"

"Not right now." His deep voice rolled around the gorge. "But I may be calling you soon."

"Any time." Ethan lifted a hand as Quinlan turned and flew straight up, his Guard falling in behind him. Ethan's forces shouted after them, cheering them on.

Samantha turned and looked at them, waving their fists, glorying in a victory over an impossible enemy. Tears sprang to her eyes.

Once they'd disappeared over the east ridge, Ethan gave orders that all the surviving wraith-pairs were to be locked up until the following night. He didn't give a reason, but it was clear to everyone that Samantha needed rest before she'd be able to help dissolve the pairs.

He glanced at Vojalie. "I'm going to take Samantha back to the house. She needs a good meal and rest."

"And a hot bath."

Ethan smiled tenderly down at her. "Yes, a nice hot bath." He even kissed her forehead. "But before we do, Vojalie, I want you to tell her the truth, tell her who you are. I don't want her learning from anyone else, but I think it's time."

"Tell me what?"

Vojalie turned her warm brown eyes on Samantha and caught her chin with her hand. "I didn't know how to tell you and though my husband can irritate the hell out of me at times, he is right about one thing: *timing is important.*

"When you first came here, you didn't know me, or anything really about our world. And to be honest, I was completely taken aback that Andrea had never even spoken of me. She was my daughter, you see, one I had before Davido and I became a couple. You and I are related."

Samantha's throat grew incredibly tight and tears fell from her eyes even though she didn't want to cry or make a fuss, but the thought that she wasn't alone in the world anymore brought the tears falling.

"Forgive me for not telling you sooner."

Samantha drew in a shaky breath. "It's okay. I understand a lot more now, after these past three days than I would have earlier. So many things make sense and no, she couldn't have told me about you, because she didn't tell me she was fae. I just thought she had really striking features." She laughed, thinking how she'd lied to herself as well.

"I want to get to know you and I hope we'll at least be able to be friends."

Samantha saw the doubt, even the fear, in her eyes, that she'd be rejected. So, despite her trembling fatigue, she reached out and took Vojalie's hand. She told her briefly what she now believed had happened to Andrea during the last year she was in Bergisson, and about the way the dark fae presence had recently interfered with Samantha's mind, giving her old visions of the massacre, confusing her.

"So, you see, Andrea just didn't know that she was being systematically injured, you might even say enthralled. I think by the time she did have a vision of what would happen here at Sweet Gorge, the night that Ethan lost his family, she couldn't take it anymore. She wrote as much in her last journal and if you'd like to read them, you're more than welcome."

Vojalie shaded her face. "If only I'd known."

"None of us knew," Ethan said. "We barely understood why the stream dried up. This ancient fae is very powerful. She has extensive enthrallment skills that she could have prevented all of us from seeing the eastern plain for the past several years, a place that Ry had used as a training camp. That's a lot of power, to have kept us all confused."

"It is," Vojalie agreed. "But apparently still not enough to help Ry and his Invictus force take over your Realm."

Ethan squeezed Samantha's waist. "I think we owe a lot of that to Samantha's courage." He smiled. "Even her cunning at times."

Vojalie looked from one to the other. "You've completed the bonding process."

"We did."

Samantha recalled the recurring daydream she'd been having since she was a child about the house by the lake, made of river-stone, and surrounded by land, and something occurred to her about how persistent that image had remained. "Vojalie, does any of your family own a house by a lake? The one I described to you not long ago?"

Vojalie's eyes filled with tears. "Your mother's home, one that belonged in my family for centuries. She lived there with Patrick."

In this moment, Samantha felt the past and the future rush together, two waves colliding and passing through each other. She stared at Vojalie, her mother's mother, her unknown grandmother.

"I've been connected all these years to Bergisson and never knew it." She held Vojalie's gaze and when her grandmother opened her arms, Samantha fell into them and held Vojalie tight.

Vojalie held her for a long time and Samantha let her.

A fae vibration sang between them. The past was made whole in this moment, life coming full circle in a beautiful, surprising way. For a long moment, Samantha felt as though her mother was right here with them.

When at last she drew back, Vojalie's brown eyes were damp. "I never thought to have a connection with my daughter again. Thank you for this, Samantha. Thank you from the depths of my heart."

Samantha nodded. She didn't want the moment to end but fatigue now worked in her. Ry's feeding had taken a toll, as well as the terrible stress of the entire situation.

"Take her home," Vojalie said.

Ethan nodded and held his arm out for Samantha. She stepped up on his foot and slid her arm around his neck. As he took her into the air, she looked back at Vojalie growing smaller and smaller as Ethan took her high into the starry night sky.

*** *** ***

Ethan had showered and wore only his navy silk robe as he tended to Samantha.

His housekeeper had prepared a light supper of potato soup, fresh sour dough bread lathered with butter, and a salad made up from greens from the kitchen garden. She'd included a bottle of imported German wine, a taste Ethan had quickly acquired once his realm had started importing from Shreveport. A lot of the mastyrs liked German wine.

He kept supplying Samantha with whatever she needed, whether another slice of bread or a refill on her wine glass, or another helping of soup. She was famished for many reasons, one of them being that Ry had taken a lot of her blood, something he tried not to think about.

"Is there any salad left?"

"Yes, of course. Plenty."

"Then I'd like more, especially any extra radicchio you find in there."

"Coming right up." He smiled. He couldn't stop smiling because he couldn't believe his good fortune. He had a woman lounging in his white, claw-foot ceramic tub, arms draped over the sides, bubbles floating over and around her, and she belonged to him.

The bond between them felt as normal now as breathing and he couldn't remember what his life had been like just a few nights ago, when he'd stormed into the prave and arrested the vampire, Tom, for illegal blood-taking at a human event.

Now he was here, picking out pieces of radicchio, because that's what his woman wanted in her salad.

Yes, *his woman.*

When he brought the salad back to her, he sat on the stool next to the tub and carefully fed her one bite at a time. Each time, she sucked the dressing off his fingers, which of course kept him in an aroused state he had difficulty disguising, especially when she'd arch her back and her tight nipples would appear from beneath sliding islands of bubbles.

He could look, but he couldn't touch. She'd set the rules, because, as she said, her body was still rebuilding her supply and she wouldn't be ready to feed him for at least another half hour.

He'd just have to wait.

She'd made the right call because he knew the moment he took her to bed he'd need to take her vein; the two acts just couldn't be separated, not tonight.

And this joining would be different from all the others because they'd completed the bond.

She took a sip of wine, then more salad.

He stroked her cheek, which she allowed. "How are you feeling?"

She smiled. "Better, but anxious to be back in bed with you. I need this as well."

He nodded. He could feel her need and it was more than just physical, as though what had happened out at Sweet Gorge required this union to be fully realized.

Finally, she'd taken her last bite and said he could towel her dry. He set aside the glasses and plates, then returned to the tub with a thick towel, aware he trembled with need, and his cock pushed at the silk of the robe. She stood up and he leaned down to hit the lever to drain the tub, then wrapped her up in the towel.

Lifting her out and onto the floor, he dried her, caressing her and kissing her at the same time, top to bottom, front to back. She giggled and cooed, and stroked his now dry hair, his face, and teased his lips with her fingers.

When he finally kissed her, he felt the solidity of the bond deep in his abdomen, as though an invisible cord stretched between them, and desire pulsed through him in heavy waves. He felt her response as she suckled his tongue, fondled his muscles, and groaned against his mouth.

He lifted her in his arms and carried her to the bed. Having had the keen foresight to roll the comforter back, he laid her out, getting rid of the towel at the same time.

"Robe. Off." She commanded, but her beautiful light blue eyes glittered with amusement.

He smiled, then laughed. She'd always been able to do that, to make him laugh, and he loved her for it, one of the many things he loved.

He stretched out on top, planting his knees between her thighs. With his forearms next to her, he thumbed her lips, then her line of her jaw. "This is a very fae chin you have."

"I guess it is, but not so pointed as my mother's."

"Do you miss her a lot, Samantha?"

"Every day. She was my best friend."

He heard the hitch in her voice. "That must have been hard for you, being alone in Shreveport."

"I'd come to accept it, maybe in the same way I feel a similar acceptance in you. But now it looks like I have a whole new family, two in fact: one with you and one with Vojalie. Oh, I just realized, Bernice is my…wait, I'm not even sure what the relationship is. She would have been my mother's sister." She giggled. "Baby Bernice is my aunt."

He smiled as well. "I'm sure this must all seem strange since from a human perspective Vojalie doesn't look much older than you."

"I suppose not, except her eyes. She looks very old, very wise in her eyes."

He leaned down and kissed her. So this was what it was to make love to a woman, to be in love, and to love. Ethan had never thought to be in this place, not for years to come, because of Bergisson and what was fast-developing as a major war against an ancient fae force and the Invictus she controlled.

Instead, his blood rose had arrived to show him a new path, a completely different journey, by which he would be able to do a better job at keeping his realm safe. Yes, he had increased power because of his bond with Samantha, but greater than that were the lessons he'd learned of allowing increased leadership among those closest to him. He had new plans for Finn and Kyle and he meant to meet with Quinlan and Gerrod within the next week to begin planning long-term strategies to force the dark fae entity, and the Great Mastyr, out into the open. And these were just two of many new ideas kicking around in his head.

But right now, he had his woman in his bed and he focused his thoughts on her, on the sweetness of her crushed raspberry-and-wine scent, the soft vibrations that emanated from the seat of her fae power, from the affection he saw reflected in her lovely light blue eyes, and in the softness of her lips.

He entered her well with reverence this time, and awe, and wonder, that so much sheer joy could be contained within a woman. He held her gaze as he thrust steadily, pushing her on and on toward her climax. He savored that she writhed beneath him when he pinned her hands above her head, and worked her strongly with his hips.

He sent his personal frequency in strong pulses against her body and watched her back arch each time the frequency pushed against her fae power.

He thrust faster, wanting to watch her come, to cry out, to experience her ecstasy. Nothing seemed more important in the entire world than this, than bringing her pleasure.

Soft cries left her lips. Her head rolled from side to side. Her eyelids fluttered.

He mover stronger now, vampire strong, and then vampire fast, using his speed to drive her straight over the edge. She cried out a long almost anguished sound as pleasure streaked through his cock in a series of intense pulses. He groaned, maybe he shouted, and all the while the bond between them tightened and intensified.

When her body eased down and his muscles started to relax he all but fell on top of her with deep satisfied.

But she smiled and stroked his cheek. "We're not done yet." She turned her head exposing a throbbing vein for him. "Now take your fill and do me again."

The site of her neck ready for him, firmed him up and as his fangs struck, he began to pump as he sucked down her erotically flavored blood once more. Her hands moved over his body, exploring his muscles, heightening his pleasure, until once more she was crying out and his shouts rang through his bedroom.

*** *** ***

Samantha lay on her back and had been in this position long after Ethan fell asleep. He'd made love to her more than once after feeding from her vein and she'd adored every second of it.

He was half-sprawled over her, his head on her chest, an arm over her stomach, and one knee on her thigh.

She wrapped and unwrapped a strand of his long hair around her finger.

She stared unseeing at the ceiling, marveling at all that had happened to her and all that in just a few short days she'd become. She'd basically endured a crash-course in how-to-be-a-fae and a powerful one at that. But she'd survived, as much because of Ethan as anything else, and she'd passed from have a fairly withdrawn view of what her life should be to now sharing a bed with a mastyr vampire, serving as his blood rose, and eventually taking her place in Bergisson as Vojalie's granddaughter.

Above all, love had come to her so miraculously that gratitude poured through her over and over, a stream of beautiful warmth that caused the crystals all the way in the conservatory to hum in response.

She'd asked Ethan to leave the doors open that she might be able to hear the crystals sing, a sound that would always remind her of the goodness that had come to her when she'd taken the risk to join Ethan in Bergisson the first night she'd met him.

She hoped the crystals would always sing.

Her eyelids fluttered and as she began to drift off to sleep, she saw the cottage again, the one of her girlish daydreams and wishes, though now she knew it had always been so much more than that, nothing short of a fae vision.

But this time, she saw her mother standing beside the cottage beckoning her forward and pathing, *I prepared this for you. The cottage belonged to one of our forebears, then to me. Now it's yours.*

Two toddlers raced by her mother, two little girls, each with long curly blond locks, and in Samantha's twilight sleep she saw Ethan's hair reflected in the girls whom she knew to belong to her in the future—her daughters.

Her faeness sang through the vision and she joined her mother as Andrea showed her the cottage by the lake, made of river-stone and landscaped with trees that touched the water.

Here, she embraced the full magic of her life.

Here she would raise her children and sing the song of gratitude forever, in the arms of the man she loved.

About The Author

Caris Roane, aka Valerie King, has published, to-date, twelve paranormal romances. As Valerie King, she's written over fifty Regency romance novels and novellas and has launched a new line of Regency books from sweet to sexy. In 2005, Romantic Times gave her a Career Achievement award in Regency Romance.

As Caris Roane, she also writes contemporary romance and has recently released her first contemporary, A SEDUCTIVE PROPOSITION.

Caris lives in Phoenix, Arizona, loves to write, really doesn't like scorpions, and has two cats, Sebastien and Gizzy.

For more information about Caris Roane: www.carisroane.com

For more information about Valerie King: www.valerieking-romance.com.

CPSIA information can be obtained
at www.ICGtesting.com
Printed in the USA
FSOW02n1102090217
30618FS

9 781494 955359